WALLFLOWER WHISPERS

WALTZING WITH WALLFLOWERS (BOOK 3)

ROSE PEARSON

LANDON HILL MEDIA

© Copyright 2024 by Rose Pearson - All rights reserved.

In no way is it legal to reproduce, duplicate, or transmit any part of this document by either electronic means or in printed format. Recording of this publication is strictly prohibited and any storage of this document is not allowed unless with written permission from the publisher. All rights reserved.

Respective author owns all copyrights not held by the publisher.

WALLFLOWER WHISPERS

hugh Blackmore
Rachael Simmons

PROLOGUE

"Have you heard?"

Miss Rachael Simmons did her best not to overhear, having tucked herself away in an alcove to recover for a short while from the heat of the ballroom.

"Are you about to tell me some delicious rumor?" the other lady said, giggling, though Rachael rolled her eyes. "Do tell me quickly! You know how much I *adore* such things as that!"

Rachael closed her eyes and leaned her head back, quite certain that she was well hidden and would not be seen. No doubt the two ladies speaking in such friendly yet conspiring tones would be shamed into silence should they discover she was nearby, though they would then simply find another place to share their gossip. Rachael herself was not inclined to either listen to, or take part in gossip, finding it both a distraction from what was being offered to her during this wonderful Season and also, to her mind, most unfavorable to whoever was being spoken about. It was never any good news that was spoken of but always dark, whispered things or, as it often turned out, fabrications that then injured whichever parties were involved.

"It is about Lord Blackmore."

Keeping her eyes closed, Rachael sighed inwardly and wondered how long it would take for the two ladies to take their leave. She would soon be required to return to her mother and father, the Viscount and Viscountess Grant, though her mother knew where she had gone, and had granted her permission to find a quiet place for a few minutes to regain her composure. After all, she had declared, the redness in Rachael's cheeks had been a little *too* bright and would deter gentlemen should they see it. A wry smile crossed her face as she shook her head, wondering at her mother's considerations. Would the color of her cheeks truly affect her chances at happiness?

"I have heard that there is a *secret* betrothal between himself and a lady of the *ton*," the first lady continued, making Rachael scowl. Lord Blackmore was one of her acquaintances - she did not know him particularly well at all, though he was certainly a reputable gentleman. Gossip would not aid him in any way at all.

"A secret betrothal, you say?" exclaimed the second, as Rachael imagined the first lady nodding fervently. "Why is it secret?"

"Because," the first lady replied, her tone lowering, "there is a *reason* for this betrothal to be secret. There cannot be any time between their betrothal and marriage, do you see?"

A prickling ran down Rachael's spine. She had no doubt what it was that this first lady was attempting to suggest, and even the thought of it made her uncomfortable.

What if there is some truth to it?

Rachael shook her head to herself, scowling in frustration. She was not about to let herself become mixed up with gossip, and would not let herself ruminate on such things. It would be fruitless.

"You do not mean to say that she is with child?"

The hissed whisper of the second lady had Rachael's hands curling tightly. Whoever this lady they gossiped about was, she prayed that the first gossiper did not know her name for, if she did, then the news would surely soon spread throughout all of London. Besides which, it might not even be true!

"That is what has been said. This young lady was seen coming out of Lord Blackmore's townhouse in the early hours of the morning, at the very beginning of the Season and, thereafter, there are whispers of a betrothal! There can only be one reason for such a thing."

"Good gracious."

Rachael swallowed hard, her brow furrowing. To have a young lady leaving his townhouse in the early morning hours did not speak well of Lord Blackmore but, then again, that in itself might also be nothing more than a rumor. Her eyes closed again.

I wish I did not have to listen to this.

"What is the name of the lady? Is it someone known to us?"

"I know *of* her," the first said, quietly. "I am not acquainted though, I must say, I am surprised to see her dancing and laughing with the gentlemen here, as though all is well."

"And does she not look as though she is with child?" the second lady asked. "There must be some altering of her appearance by now, surely?"

"There are ways to keep such things hidden for a long time." The answer was given with some authority, as though she knew precisely what she was talking about. "No doubt she will soon have to take her leave of London, though once the betrothal is announced, it will simply seem as though she is returning to her father's estate for her preparations before her wedding – though no doubt it will also be to hide the fact that she is increasing from the *ton*."

"Goodness!" The shock in the voice of the second lady made Rachael scowl. Why was she so quick to believe the first? Surely there would be some questions in her mind, some wondering as to whether or not such a thing would be true? "What is the name of this unfortunate lady, then? *Do* tell me! You cannot keep such a thing to yourself."

The first laughed softly.

"Very well, I shall tell you. The name of the lady is one Miss Rachael Simmons. She is the daughter of Viscount Grant – he is here this very evening, which means she must be present also! I cannot imagine what she thinks she is doing at present, behaving as she does when she is with child! If it were me, then I think I would be hiding myself away from society rather than parading myself about!"

Rachael blinked, the words coming to her slowly,

their impact gradually beginning to deaden her heart as she took them in, one phrase at a time.

They are speaking about... me?

It was not possible, surely? Why would they be speaking of her? She had no connection to Lord Blackmore, no interest in his company or even in acquainting herself further with him! She had certainly not left his townhouse at an early hour of the morning – in fact, she had never set foot in his townhouse! So why now were people suggesting that *she* was the one who had done such a thing?

"*She* is with child? Goodness, how could such a thing be!"

Before she knew what was happening, Rachael found herself on her feet, rounding on the two ladies who, their faces going white with shock, stared back at her.

"I am *not* with child!" she exclaimed, throwing up her hands, her voice carrying more than she realized. "I am acquainted with Lord Blackmore, yes, but I have never once visited his townhouse, *nor* have I departed from it in the early hours of the morning! This is disgraceful! It is despicable to speak such lies about me! How dare you do such a thing?"

The first lady blinked rapidly, her mouth slack. The second, however, immediately began to stammer.

"We... we mean no harm, Miss... Miss Simmons. Really, we do not. Miss Featheringham is only repeating what she has heard from someone else."

"And who might this someone else be?" Rachael demanded, turning now to face the first lady who was still terribly overcome with shock, though Rachael did not care in the least. "Who did you hear this from?"

"I – I do not recall." The first lady, someone Rachael was not at all acquainted with, stepped back from her, her blue eyes wide and staring. "I did not mean to–"

"Well, once you recall who it is, you will go to them at once and state that you have heard directly from me that there is *no* child present and that the rumors are entirely untrue. Do you understand what this will do to my reputation? What it will do to my chances of a successful match?" Fear clutched her heart and Rachael dropped her hands to her sides, squeezing her eyes closed as a sudden weakness rocked her frame. "I will be thrown from society! I will no longer have any standing! I will be disgraced and ignored and all because of some foolish rumor which has no truth in it whatsoever!" She shuddered, her voice dropping to a whisper. "What have you done?"

Silence came from the two ladies. They looked at each other and then back to Rachael as she opened her eyes, a great and terrible fear grasping her. Was this to be the end of her London Season? Was she to lose all hope of finding and securing a match? This rumor, wherever it had come from, would ruin her standing in society, and would tarnish her name and have her disgraced, even though no word of what was being said was true!

"We will tell everyone that it is *not* true," the second lady said, grasping Rachael's hand tightly. "We will inform them that there is no truth to this rumor, and that is all it is – a rumor."

Rachael shook her head and swallowed hard.

"I appreciate your willingness to make amends, but I am certain that there will still be damage done." Her voice was thick with grief, pain racing through her words. "You do not know where you heard such a rumor and thus, I must now believe that it will be spread about through London, and I will find myself never able to return." She said this looking at the first lady again, but Miss Featheringham did not answer her with a response of anything more than a shrug. Either she was truly entirely unaware of who it was who had offered her this particular rumor, *or* she was protecting them by refusing to say. Whatever the reason, Rachael felt as if she were being pulled into the depths of despair, into a low pit that would slowly pull away every single bit of light from her.

"We will do our best," the second lady reassured her, as Rachael slumped back against the wall, her vision blurring, her heart beating painfully as her strength began to leave her. "Hopefully it will pass."

"It will not," Rachael whispered, her eyes closing as dampness clung to her lashes.

Something as severe as this, she knew, would not simply fade away like the shadows of the night into the morning. Instead, it would linger, leaving an indelible stain that would forever cling to her.

There would be nothing for her now.

CHAPTER ONE

One year later.

Hugh Hampden, Earl of Blackmore, sighed and leaned back in his chair. There was still quite a bit of business for him to deal with this morning, and he was already fatigued. It would be much easier if he went to London to deal with certain things in person but, at the moment, caution kept him at his estate. After the fiasco of last year's Season, he did not want to return. He did not want to make his way back to where so many whispers and dark words circulated. His younger brother had thought to come to London this Season also, but Hugh did not think it would be wise for him to make an appearance - not when there were so many whispers still. For the moment, Hugh had advised that it would be better for him to remain in Bath.

There came a tap at the door.

"Yes?" When the butler walked in, Hugh lifted an eyebrow. "Well?"

Disliking being interrupted when he was hard at

work, his mind filled with numbers and names, Hugh did his best to keep his irritation from his voice.

"My Lord, you have a visitor."

Hugh blinked.

"A visitor?"

"Yes, my Lord. He states that he is aware that his arrival is unexpected, but he has come nonetheless."

Still a little surprised that someone had come to his estate to call on him, Hugh nodded.

"Very well. Who is it who has come to call?"

"Lord Elmsford, my Lord." The butler stepped forward to hand Hugh the gentleman's card, but Hugh was already half out of his chair, surprise and delight racing through him.

"Lord Elmsford is here? Then show him in! Show him in at once!" The butler obliged and a broad smile transformed Hugh's face as he greeted his friend. "Elmsford! Whatever are you doing here?" Shaking the gentleman's hand firmly, he gestured for him to come a little further into the study. "Not that you are unwelcome, of course! I am very glad to see you."

"I am relieved." Lord Elmsford chuckled and slapped Hugh on the shoulder, a sign of the long friendship they had enjoyed ever since they had been young boys at Eton together. "It would have been a great trial to me to have traveled all of this way, only to find that my friend has no desire to see me!"

"No, indeed. I truly am very happy that you have come, though I suspect, knowing you, that there is a purpose behind your visit? You have not come simply to call upon me for a brief while."

Lord Elmsford nodded though his smile remained.

"You are correct, there *is* something which I wish to say, though it does not have to be said immediately."

"Of course. You are fatigued from your journey, I am sure. Shall I send for a tea tray? You will stay for a few days, I hope?

With a smile, Lord Elmsford settled himself into a comfortable chair.

"I will not refuse that offer – on both counts! I will accept a tea tray, perhaps a measure of brandy to go with it and a few days of residing with you would be very much appreciated – though I hope that you will return with me when it comes time for me to take my leave."

Hugh frowned, going across the room to ring the bell, though the butler returned almost immediately. Telling the man that Lord Elmsford was to stay for a few days and that they required refreshments, Hugh dismissed him and then returned his attention to Lord Elmsford.

"Returning with you?" he asked, as Lord Elmsford nodded. "Why should I do that? Your estate is far from here and–"

"I intend to go to London for the Season," Lord Elmsford interrupted, making Hugh's frown deepen all the more. "And I was hoping that I might be able to convince you to return with me." He let out a small sigh and shook his head. "That, in short, is what I have come to say. Your friends and I all wish for you to return to London. It is not the same without your company!"

A hint of a smile lifted one corner of Hugh's mouth, but he pulled it back quickly.

"I have no desire to come to London this Season,

although I appreciate that all of you seek my company. It is considerate of you to come to my estate to encourage me to return but, in truth, I should prefer to remain here." That was not entirely true, and Hugh felt a twinge of shame run through him, though he cleared his throat and shrugged to hide it. "I have a good deal of business to attend to."

"Much of which could be done in London," his friend replied, easily. "I know that as well as you. You need not hide the truth from me, old friend. I am all too aware of what it is that troubles you."

Hugh grimaced but said nothing. The refreshments arrived and, as they were set out, Hugh let himself consider what Lord Elmsford had suggested, though immediately there came with it a sense of foreboding. Sighing and seeing his friend's look of curiosity, he shook his head.

"I do not think that I can return to London this Season," he said, eventually. "I do not want to go back to a place where all of society thinks me the very worst sort of gentleman!"

"But that rumor has been proven false, has it not?" Lord Elmsford pointed out. "The young lady in question remained in London for the entirety of the Season and thereafter, was seen at many other social occasions – though she became something of a wallflower in the end unfortunately – and it was clear to everyone that there was no child. Your betrothal to her was whispered about also, yes, but that only required you to speak of your lack of connection to her."

Heat built in Hugh's chest.

"All the same, to hear such things whispered about me, to know that the *ton* believed that I was responsible for such things, was difficult indeed."

"And you think that another year at home, another Season without your presence will aid that?"

"How could it not?" Hugh asked, pouring the coffee for himself and his friend. "Within another year, the rumors and whispers will have faded away and gone to something else entirely."

"Only to rise again with a great strength when you finally do return," Lord Elmsford finished, making Hugh grimace. "That is why I have come to speak with you. The rumors from last Season might have been blown out but there is still smoke present. This year, there are still rumors snaking their way through society." Taking a sip of his coffee, he set his cup down carefully and then looked back at Hugh. "What is being said now is that, although Miss Simmons was not with child, there *was* a young lady who stepped away from your townhouse in the early hours of the morning last Season. The *ton* simply does not know who it is as yet. Some say it *was*, in fact, Miss Simmons."

Hugh, who had been taking a sip of his coffee as his friend spoke, spluttered violently, setting his cup down and pulling out his handkerchief instead.

"What?" he demanded, once he had wiped his mouth, his eyes staring hard at his friend. "That cannot be true, surely? Why would they say such things as that?"

"Because you are not in London." With a wry look, Lord Elmsford spread out his hands. "You are not at the London Season and thus, people believe that you are deliberately hiding away *because* of your guilt. You must return to London. You must hold your head high and make your way through society as you have always done. That is the only way to remove such rumors from yourself entirely."

Hugh passed one hand over his eyes, sighing heavily.

"It pains me to have to do such a thing as that. I would much prefer a quieter life rather than have to do this and that to prove my innocence to the *ton*."

"How quiet a life would you wish it to be?" Lord Elmsford scowled. "You are aware that, should you continue to do as you wish and remain here, then your name and your reputation could easily be sullied and that could linger for many a year. Perhaps even to your heir."

Lord Elmsford scowled.

"I have no heir."

"Not as yet," his friend agreed, "but that is something you require and, no doubt, something you will gain at some point in this life. Would you truly be contented if your child were to be born and, thereafter, have his name already darkened by a past stain?" He spread out his hands. "Even though you have done nothing wrong? Would it not be best to face it now, to come back to society and to make it quite clear that you have nothing to be ashamed of?"

Hugh sighed and ran one hand over his eyes.

"Is it truly as serious as that?"

A heaviness settled in his stomach as his friend nodded, never once lifting his gaze, or letting a hint of a smile touch his expression. If Lord Elmsford had come all of this way, had come to call on him to bring him back to

London, then mayhap it *was* a good deal more serious than Hugh had at first thought.

"I will not force your hand, but I wanted you to know of my concerns, given that I am your friend." Lord Elmsford reached out and picked up a cake from the tray, setting it on a plate, clearly hungry. "I will stay for a day or two and then return to London. It is my hope that you will join me."

Hugh harrumphed.

"I do not wish to go to London," he said again, making his friend grin ruefully. "What of the unfortunate young lady?"

"Of Miss Simmons?"

Nodding, Hugh frowned and looked away.

"I was acquainted with her, of course, but we were never very closely acquainted. To hear that she was the one who had supposedly been caught escaping from my house in the early hours of the morning made me so very embarrassed. I had to pray that she did not think that *I* had been the one to put her name to it."

"I do not think that you need to have any embarrassment whatsoever," came the reply, though there was a shadow in Lord Elmsford's voice that Hugh had not expected to hear. "She did not think anything of you, I am sure. Her shame was enough to bear."

A nudge of guilt pressed into Hugh's heart, and he looked away again, realizing too late that he had been thinking solely of himself, and what Miss Simmons might think of *him*. He had not been thinking, instead, of the suffering which Miss Simmons herself might have endured.

"I presume she is not back in London?"

"Miss Simmons? No, not as far as I have seen. I would not expect her to be present, not after such a great and terrible rumor as that has been set on her shoulders."

"But she has proven it to be false!" Hugh exclaimed as Lord Elmsford shrugged. "That seems deeply unfair. Why should a young lady be punished for what is nothing more than a rumor – and a false one at that?"

His friend tilted his head.

"That is something which mayhap you, yourself, can address when you come to London."

Hugh rolled his eyes and laughed, even though his own heart and mind were deeply unsettled.

"That is an interesting way of attempting to encourage me to return to town."

"It would be good for both yourself *and* for Miss Simmons," his friend stated, firmly. "Even if she does not return to London, your presence in town and your attempts to quash all of the rumors will be of aid to her, I am sure. I, and your other friends, will aid you in this; we will say the very same thing as you and pray that the *ton* pays attention to all of us. That way, your name will be lifted to its rightful position and the *ton* might forget entirely about Miss Simmons, who will then be able to step forward in confidence rather than be forced to cling to the shadows."

Letting out a long, slow breath, Hugh shook his head.

"You do make some very convincing arguments, my friend."

"Convincing enough to encourage you to do as I have

suggested?" A light came into Lord Elmsford's eyes. "Will you come with me back to London?"

"I will consider it." Not all that easily convinced, Hugh smiled as Lord Elmsford's face fell. "There is much I must think on, though I will say that I am grateful to you for what you have done in coming to me, and speaking to me of all of this." His smile faded. "I would not have known of any of it – nor the whispers which continue to grow – had you not come."

Lord Elmsford smiled.

"I came also for your brandy, given that you find the very best French brandy in all of England."

Hugh snorted with laughter, the tension and strain disappearing already.

"Then you must have as much of it as you like these next few days," he said, making his friend grin. "Though I truly am grateful. It has given me much to think on."

Returning to London was not something that Hugh had even considered these last few months. To his mind, it had been nothing more than a thought – and one that he had tossed aside hastily thereafter. Now, however, Lord Elmsford's concerns were forcing him to reconsider. He did not want his name to be splattered with the muddy whispers of the *ton*. Lord Elmsford was quite right that it could very well pass on to his heir, should he live to have one, and that was a great concern to him. Sighing inwardly, Hugh rubbed his chin and turned his gaze to the window. Even though he was loath to do so, even though the entirety of his desire was to remain at his estate, it seemed now as though he had no other choice.

He would return to London.

CHAPTER TWO

"There is no hope, Father."

Rachael looked around the ballroom and saw how the eyes that turned in her direction quickly pulled away again, only for hands to raise to mouths which, behind those hands, no doubt immediately began to whisper about her. Tears began to burn in her eyes, but her father settled one hand on her shoulder, his quiet smile an attempt to be encouraging.

"Do not give up hope yet, my dear. We have come back to London, aware that we have already proven that the rumors from last Season were nothing but a falsehood. Why should you be punished for something that was clearly untrue?"

"Because the *ton* has decided that I must be." Miserable, Rachael dropped her head and closed her eyes tightly against her tears. "It will do no good, being here. If it is already said that I bear some shame, even if it is not true, the rumors have already spread widely enough to damage my reputation."

"It is most unfair." With a small sigh, Lady Grant put one arm around Rachael's waist and pulled her close. "But we are not ready to give up, not as yet! We have come to London to prove to the *ton* that you have nothing to hide from. Whether it will do any good remains to be seen, but I must hope that, by the end of the Season, you will have regained your social standing."

Rachael looked up at her mother, trying to find the same sort of hope within her own heart as was in her mother's voice and expression, but there was nothing but a heavy sadness there instead. This was her first ball of the Season, the first time that she had been out in society, and while it seemed that the invitations were not slow in coming to her father's townhouse, stepping *into* the room had not brought her the same welcome.

"You should walk with Father around the ballroom, Mama," Rachael suggested, her voice quiet but determined, even though her mother quickly shook her head. "It will be good for you both to be seen, and I am sure that many a friend or acquaintance will wish to speak with you. If I am with you, then perhaps that will not be so."

Her father immediately shook his head.

"We cannot leave you standing at the side of the ballroom without a chaperone. It would not be proper."

"I will stand with the other wallflowers," Rachael replied, gesturing to the three who had gathered there and, catching the eye of one of them, smiling back at her. "I consider them my friends, Father, since we became so well-known to each other last Season. I will be quite safe and, given that I must also consider myself a wallflower now, no one will so much as look at me."

"You are not a wallflower, Rachael!" Lady Grant sounded so utterly horrified, Rachael could not help but smile, albeit sadly. "You must not think of yourself so."

"I will think of myself as I must," she answered, softly. "Go, Mama. Walk about the ballroom, greet your friends and mayhap, as you have said, it will lead to the regaining of my social standing by the end of the Season itself." She glanced again at the other wallflowers. "I will go to them."

She watched as her mother and father exchanged a look. It did not take long, however, for her father to agree to Rachael's suggestion, though he did make her promise that she would not move from where she stood with the wallflowers, *and* swore that they would be but a few minutes. Relieved, Rachael watched them take their leave of her and then, turning, hurried to her friends.

"Good evening, Miss Simmons!" Lady Frederica stepped forward, grasping her hands. "I did not know if you would come to London this Season, but I am very glad indeed to see you again. How are you at present?"

Rachael looked from one friend to the other, her shoulders dropping.

"I would say that I am well and, whilst that would be true, it would not express the sorrows of my heart at the clear dislike which is etched upon the faces of so many people present this evening."

"Which is utterly ridiculous, given that you have done nothing worthy of their dislike." Miss Fairley shook her head and clicked her tongue, looking away. "It is nothing but a sham, this business of being a wallflower. I do not like it in the least."

"I do not think that any wallflower is particularly contented with being a wallflower," Rachael replied, with a wry smile. "Though I will say that I am glad to see you all again. That has given me a little more hope, at least."

Lady Frederica tilted her head.

"Hope?"

With a wry smile, Rachael lifted her shoulders.

"My mother hopes that I will be able to regain my social standing by the end of the Season. She is praying that the *ton* will forget all about what they have placed upon me and that, by the end of the Season, I will be just as any other young lady."

Lady Frederica's gaze sharpened.

"I can tell from your expression that you do not feel the same."

"Is it so very apparent?" With a wry look, Rachael turned her head and gestured to the other guests. "One thing I have learned is that the *ton* has very long memories and tightly grasping hands. If they wish to, they will hold onto these rumors, listen long to the whispers about me, and hold it close to them for as long as they please. I do not think, therefore, that it will be as easy as my mother believes. I do not think that the *ton* will forget about what they think of me simply because I am present in London. Indeed, they will, no doubt, think all the worse of me because, in seeing me again, the rumors from last Season will resurface all over again." Looking back at her friends, she searched each one for even a flicker of hope, for something that went against what she had said, but there was nothing except gentle acknowledgment written on each one's face. That was the trouble, Rachael realized. They were all pushed down and held back by the heavy tide of the *ton*'s opinion. There was nothing that they could do, nothing that would be of any help to them. They could not turn back the opinion of the *ton*, could not, simply by their presence alone, have the *ton* believe that there was no guilt upon their shoulders whatsoever. All they could do instead was simply watch what went by and silently pray that, one day soon, their supposed shame would be forgotten, and they could return to their positions in society, as they had been before.

The chance of that happening was slim.

"And have you seen Lord Blackmore as yet?"

Rachael shook her head.

"It is so very strange. I did not know the gentleman very well at all! We were acquainted, yes, and I believed we had danced on one occasion, but that was all. We were not so closely connected to have the *ton* believe there was anything of interest between us. Why my name should then be connected with his, why *I* should be the one whom it was suggested had done such a heinous thing as what was said, and why, thereafter, it was said that we were betrothed, is quite beyond me. I have done nothing to encourage a close connection between myself and Lord Blackmore and yet, for some reason, someone believed that I was the young lady who had stepped out of his townhouse early in the morning!" She shook her head and tried to ignore the stab of pain that came with her words. "It was all utterly preposterous and yet, society believed it without question."

"Not everyone did," Miss Fairley murmured, gently. "We did not."

"And I am grateful to all of you for that," Rachael answered, putting one hand to her heart. "In truth, if I had not discovered you last Season, then I do not know what I would have done. I think I would have broken apart from loneliness!"

Miss Fairley smiled in understanding.

"I feel the same. We are all connected, all supporting each other through what are very difficult circumstances. No doubt more young ladies will join us, and we will be able to offer the same support to them. How unfair it is that society treats us so! We ought to be able to go about in society just as they do, given that none of what has been placed upon us is our own doing!"

"That is true," Rachael murmured, wondering how one would go about such a thing. "The *ton* seems to believe that, even though I was clearly not with child, there is still some great shame attached to me. Some believe that I was sent away from Lord Blackmore's house in those early hours, that even though I was not with child, I was still in his company for that particular length of time which is quite ridiculous. Others, I think, simply believe that there is a stain upon me, though they are not quite certain what that particular stain is."

"And Lord Blackmore did not seem to have anywhere near the same burden to carry," Lady Frederica added, making Rachael wince. "He was still able to go about amongst the *ton,* able to stand up and dance at any ball he wished."

"Yes, he was." The unfairness of it all bit hard and Rachael scowled. "I do not know why such a thing should be. My own father has identified the very same but though we have pondered it, there seems to be nothing we can do. I—"

Her words were cut short as her eyes went to the very gentleman she had been speaking of. None other than Lord Blackmore himself strolled through the ballroom, walking alongside another gentleman, and with such a look of calmness on his face, Rachael wanted to scream. There was a lightness in his step, a steadiness to his expression, and a glint in his eye that spoke of contentment, of happiness and joy – and anger began to burn in the pit of her stomach.

Why was it that the *ton* could be so forgiving of *this* gentleman? A man who, though he had been proven not to have done anything wrong as regarded her, was still whispered about - but *he* was not pushed to the back of society, was not ignored and looked down upon. Was it because of his title? Because of his social standing? Or simply because he was a gentleman and she, a lady?

Her eyes closed tightly to shut out the sight, her hands curling up into tight fists, her fingernails biting into her skin.

"You have seen Lord Blackmore."

"I have." Opening her eyes, Rachael looked to Miss Fairley. "Why is it that he does not suffer in the same way as I do? Why is it that society deems him to be just as he was before? Why do they welcome him but shun me?"

"I do not know." Miss Fairley shook her head, her eyes glistening with a hint of tears. "It is the same no matter who or where we are. It seems that the gentlemen of the *ton* are given the freedom to do whatever they wish and will be, on the whole, welcomed back to society without so much as a raised eyebrow!"

"They even tolerate rogues and scoundrels," Lady Frederica sighed, "so long as they are handsome and with a good fortune. We, unfortunately, are not so fortunate."

"Indeed." Rachael turned her attention back towards Lord Blackmore, watching him laugh at something his friend had said and finding her own heart twisting with sudden resentment. Why should he continue just as usual while she was forced to linger in the shadows?

Before she could even think about what she was doing, Rachael began to make her way forward, her steps quick and hurried. She saw the very moment that Lord Blackmore set his eyes on her, for he not only came to something of a stop, but his eyes flared wide and the smile which had been on his lips began to fade.

"Good evening, Lord Blackmore."

Rachael swallowed quickly as she curtsied, not at all certain why she had stopped the gentleman, or what it was she wanted to say to him. Her feet had taken her out here and had guided her out into his path, and now that they were facing each other, she was going to have to find something to say. Something more than just a mere greeting.

"It is Miss Simmons, is it not?" Lord Blackmore cleared his throat and then gestured to his companion.

"This is Lord Elmsford, my very good friend. Lord Elmsford, this is Miss Simmons."

The way in which the gentleman's eyes flashed with interest told Rachael that he already knew precisely who she was.

"Good evening, Miss Simmons. I am glad to make your acquaintance."

She managed a smile.

"Of course." Turning her attention back to Lord Blackmore, Rachael lifted her chin. "Lord Blackmore, might I ask what it is you intend to do about this situation?"

"Do?" The gentleman blinked and then glanced at his friend. "There is nothing which concerns me at present, Miss Simmons. I am doing my best to quash the rumors which still roll around society and thus far, I believe I am doing quite well."

Rachael frowned, her eyes settling on him, taking in every part of his expression, trying to read a little more in his face than he was giving away. Lord Blackmore was not unhandsome, with dark green eyes which, at present, were looking back at her with hints of confusion swirling through them. Light brown hair swept neatly across his forehead, his firm jaw and Roman nose giving him a particularly distinguished air. His expression, however, was rather vacant as though he truly did not understand in the least what she was talking about. When he looked back at her, his eyes searching hers, Rachael found a slight heat begin to rise in her core, though she put it down to the frustration and irritation which was beginning to form.

"You speak of squashing these rumors, Lord Blackmore?" Her eyebrow lifted. "What rumors is it that you speak of, might I ask? There have been a few of late and I should like to be quite certain that we are both speaking of the same ones."

Lord Blackmore frowned.

"Why, the ones which are circulating at present, Miss Simmons."

"Which are?"

The irritation grew all the more quickly as the gentleman sighed, clearly now a little frustrated that she was continuing to press him.

"The ones which suggest that I did something disreputable last Season," he told her, looking to Lord Elmsford who nodded fervently as if to confirm this was all quite true "The ones which state that the reason I was not in London was because of my guilt, because I *did* have something to hide. None of that is true, of course, and thus I am returned to town to make certain that these rumors are quashed. Thankfully, I believe the rumor about our supposed betrothal is mostly vanquished."

Rachael's shoulders dropped.

"You seek, then, only to make the best of the situation for yourself?"

Lord Blackmore looked back at her steadily.

"But of course. Why should I not?"

"You have no concern for me, then." The gentleman's eyes widened as though he had only just realized that she too was suffering at present, and he began to cough, his words sticking in his throat and refusing to dislodge themselves. Rachael waited patiently, her hands going to her hips as Lord Blackmore continued to try to find words to explain himself. No words came. "In case you have forgotten, Lord Blackmore, I am the young lady who, it is said, left your townhouse in the very early morning one day last Season. While it has become quite clear that the second part of that particular rumor is untrue, there are still whispers over my conduct. This does not seem to concern you in the least, I presume? You have returned to London to make certain that *you* are as removed from these rumors as you can be whereas I, who have done nothing wrong either, must continue to be tormented by society's disdain!"

Lord Blackmore spread out his hands wide, his eyes still a little rounded.

"My dear Miss Simmons, I do not know what it is that you expect me to do!"

That had Rachael faltering. The truth of it was, she did *not* know what it was that she was meant to do now, or what it was that she had expected from Lord Blackmore. Coming over to him had been an action taken completely on impulse. She had been upset to see him walking through the ballroom without a care while she was forced back to stand with the other wallflowers and, without consideration, had gone to speak with him.

"I want to be considered."

That was all she could think to say, but she said it with a confidence that had Lord Blackmore's expression changing into one of understanding. Nodding, he looked away and let his hands fall to his sides.

"I understand the difficulties that come with rumors," he said, though Rachael did not immediately agree with this. "You want the *ton* to look at you in the very same way as they did before, especially since there is no truth in what you are being accused of."

Rachael, a little surprised at how well he had described it, nodded.

"Yes, that is just so. Though there is a difference between us, Lord Blackmore."

His green eyes shifted back to hers and something like a spark tumbled down her spine.

"You are able to walk through society without any great concern," she continued, hearing how her voice was a little higher than before, but putting that down solely to her frustrations and upset. "I, however, am forced back into the shadows. I have to stand with the other wallflowers – none of whom deserve to be there, I should add – even though I have no reason to be hidden away. This rumor, and what has come from it, is more significant than you might think. Not only am I now a wallflower, I have lost almost all hope of making a suitable match. After all, which gentleman would wish to marry a wallflower? Which would look upon us? To any gentleman's mind, there must be a reason for my clinging to the shadows and, should they ask, I do not doubt that they would be told of what was said of me. Even though they will be told that the whispers about a child were proven false, I do not doubt that even the *thought* of having such whispers spoken about me will be enough to drive any gentleman away. You may have lost a little of your reputation, Lord Blackmore, but you will be able to gain it back, quickly enough. I, however, have lost something a great deal more valuable, and I simply *cannot* do anything to regain it. You may be a little affected, but I am sorely affected – and can do nothing about my changed circumstances."

Lord Blackmore frowned though his gaze still held to hers.

"Be that as it may – and I am sorry for it, Miss Simmons – there is nothing that I think I can do."

Desperation began to grow in her heart and Rachael moved closer, seeing Lord Blackmore's eyes grow all the larger.

"I think that there is something which can be done," she said, softly. "You might seek to quash these rumors about your own self, Lord Blackmore but, in your attempts, might you not seek to do the same for me? Might you not mention my name? Tell those you are acquainted with how sorry you are that my name has been brought into these rumors when you are barely acquainted with me? Even a few words from you might make all of the difference."

"I am certain I could try." With a shrug, Lord Blackmore pulled his gaze away, giving Rachael the impression that he was now at the end of his conversation and was a little dulled by what she had to say. After all, there was no fervency in his reply, no great eagerness that spoke of a desire to be of aid to her. Rachael's shoulders rounded, her heart heavy and, without so much as another word to him, she turned and made her way back to her companions. Lord Blackmore spoke her name, but she did not turn her head, did not so much as glance at him. Instead, she kept her gaze upon the wall where the wallflowers stood, her heart heavy with a pain that would not seem to soften. Lord Blackmore had not given her even a thought. Even though their names had been connected to the rumor, he had decided to return to London and to do what he could for his *own* benefit, never once thinking of her, and what she must be suffering. Yes, they were not well acquainted but, as they had spoken, there had come a faint hope that he might be able to help her, might be able to encourage the *ton* to return her to her proper standing.

It seemed that hope had been nothing more than a whisper, gone in a moment. Lord Blackmore did not have any great desire to aid her and now, save for her friends, Rachael felt herself to be entirely alone.

CHAPTER THREE

"Was that Miss Simmons I saw you speaking with, Lord Blackmore?"

Hugh cleared his throat.

"Yes, Miss Wilson. It was."

He looked steadfastly at the young lady as though daring her to say anything about their meeting, but Miss Wilson only shrugged, then smiled at him.

"I could barely believe my ears when I was told that she would return to London for the Season!" Miss Wilson continued, looking at the small group of gentlemen and ladies who had gathered. "It is *very* bold of her, is it not?"

An uncomfortable prickling ran down Hugh's spine. Was this not what Miss Simmons had just come to speak with him about? And what was he going to do now? How would he respond? Would he simply stand here, and allow Miss Wilson to speak in such a way without saying a single word?

"It is *very* bold of her... as it is of someone else, I might add."

Another lady, a tall, rather formidable-looking woman whom Hugh knew to be the Marchioness of Hastings, sent a narrowed gaze towards Hugh, who immediately began to burn with a red-hot heat of annoyance.

"I have no qualms in returning to London, Lady Hastings," he said quickly, all thought of Miss Simmons removing itself from his mind. "There is nothing I have done which requires me to keep myself back from society."

Lady Hastings snorted and rolled her eyes, making her feelings quite clear.

"Is that so?"

"It is," Hugh replied firmly, though he did not miss the way that Lady Hastings' eyes narrowed in his direction. "Rumors can be a dreadful thing, Lady Hastings, for even though there is no truth to them, they can still cling with tight fingers to the person in the middle of them. I do not know where such a rumor came from, but I can assure you, I am as honorable a gentleman as you might ever find."

"I can agree with that," Lord Elmsford added, quickly, though this did not wipe the scowl from Lady Hastings' face. "When I first heard the rumor, I must confess that I laughed aloud upon hearing it! It was too ridiculous to believe."

"Of course it was." Miss Wilson smiled warmly, though her eyes darted to Lady Hastings, as though fearful of her disapprobation. "Whoever it was that witnessed Miss Simmons leaving whatever townhouse it was must have mistaken your townhouse for that of another."

The prickling returned to Hugh's spine.

"I do not think that Miss Simmons –"

"She ought not to be in London," another lady sniffed. "It is not right."

"You are quite correct, Lady Joceline," Lady Galbraith agreed, as her husband nodded silently beside her. "A lady who has done such a thing as that should either be kept back from society and required then to become a companion or some such thing, *or* she ought to be married to whoever Lord Grant can find. Thank heavens you did not agree to the betrothal, Lord Blackmore! You would have had to shoulder a substantial burden."

Hugh shook his head, tension grasping his heart and squeezing it hard.

"I must interrupt you all and state, quite clearly, that–"

"The rumors about my daughter are entirely untrue!"

A deep voice interrupted the conversation before Hugh could say anything and, twisting his head, Hugh looked into the face of Lord Grant, a gentleman he had been introduced to last Season. The man was almost purple with rage, his eyes dark and jumping from one face to the next, though his voice was controlled.

"My daughter did not behave as these rumors state," he said, his jaw tight. "That is all they are: rumors. I do not know from whence they have come, but I am determined to rid society of them! Lord Blackmore, I am sure, will concede that my daughter did not *once* step foot in his townhouse last Season and certainly did not leave it at such an early hour! As you are all aware, there is no child, there is no wrongdoing, and such shame ought not to be placed upon my daughter's shoulders any longer. It is entirely unfair."

Lady Grant put a hand to her husband's arm though, as she looked around the group, Hugh saw the gentle shimmer in her eyes. Clearly, Lady Grant was as sorrowful, as upset, as her husband on this matter. He could not imagine the suffering they must be enduring at present.

I should have said something before now.

Hugh took a small step forward.

"It was just as I was going to say, Lord Grant," he said, with a nod to the gentleman. "I was about to suggest to the assembled group that if they are willing to believe my words, that I have done nothing worthy of censure, then they ought to consider the very same as regards Miss Simmons. After all, she states that she has done nothing wrong, that the rumors are simply rumors - but society, it seems, has deemed her guilty. If you are willing to speak with me, associate with me, then why should you not do the same for her?"

Silence fell across the group and, though Hugh tried his best to keep a pleasant expression on his face, he was met with frowns and scowls rather than anyone nodding in agreement or showing the least bit of interest in what he had to say.

His heart sank.

"A young lady is not spoken of in such a way without her having done *something* akin to what is being whispered about. At least that is my experience." The Marchioness of Hastings drew herself up to her full height and glared at Lord Grant, perhaps aware that the gentleman was about to retort towards her at once. "You will, of course, believe your daughter, given that she is your daughter and, no doubt, has been able to convince you that she has done no such thing." With a mocking laugh, the Marchioness waved one hand in Lord and Lady Grant's direction. "It is not something that you should feel sorrow or regret over for, of course, it is what every parent wishes to do. However, once that has been set aside, once those of us who are *not* her family have heard of the matter, there is – reasonably, I think – a question in our minds as to the young lady's character."

"I can assure you, Lady Hastings–"

"You may assure me as much as you wish, Lady Grant, but I will make my own judgments in this," the Marchioness interrupted. "Your daughter may not be with child but to my mind, something has taken place that is worthy of censure. Others in society may not have the same opinion as I, and they may be willing to accept her company again. However, I, and my daughter, will do no such thing."

Hugh rubbed one hand over his jaw, catching the desperate look Lady Grant sent in his direction. It was all so very confusing, and yet he could see the unfairness of it all.

"But you will be in my company, Lady Hastings?"

For whatever reason, her smile spread right across her face and her eyes warmed.

"Yes, Lord Blackmore, I shall be. You are an

upstanding gentleman, and do not forget that I was acquainted with your father! Whoever reported on Miss Simmons must have mistaken the townhouse for yours, as Miss Wilson suggested."

What am I to say to that? Hugh looked back to Lady Grant, lifting his shoulders just a little and then letting them fall again. Lady Grant shook her head but then lifted her gaze and looked directly at Lady Hastings.

"My daughter was with me on the evening that this rumor began," she said, looking steadily at Lady Hastings. "Unless it is that you think that I am as much of a liar as my daughter."

Lady Hastings narrowed her gaze just a little.

"I believe that a mother would say anything to remove any hint of shame from her child," she said, coldly. "Now, do excuse me. I must return to my daughter, now that she is finished dancing with Lord Wilcox."

The group quickly dispersed as if, with Lady Hastings taking her leave, the rest of them were required now to do the same. Hugh, pausing for a moment, made to step forward, closer to Lord and Lady Grant, but the gentleman was clearly too angry to speak. With a jerky nod, he turned on his heel, away from Hugh, and his wife followed him, though she sent a brief, tight smile back in Hugh's direction first.

"At least you said something."

Hugh turned to his friend and grimaced.

"It was not done well. I should have spoken sooner. I should have spoken with greater clarity."

Lord Elmsford did not disagree, and Hugh winced, passing one hand over his eyes.

"As I have said, you spoke up when you could have remained silent, and that was well done, at the very least."

"I thank you." Speaking with a great irony filling his voice, Hugh shot Lord Elmsford a quick look. "Perhaps there is more that I can do. More I *should* do."

"And what would that be?"

Thinking quickly, Hugh waited for some idea to strike him, something obvious and actionable, but nothing came. Looking around the ballroom, he paused for a moment, his eyes catching the small group of wallflowers as they stood together, huddled as though they were helping to protect one another from the cold, icy glares of the *ton*.

"I – I should dance with her."

Lord Elmsford blinked.

"I beg your pardon?"

"I should dance with her. And you should too!" The first threads of an idea began to come to him, and he nodded to himself, smiling broadly now. "Yes, that is what must be done. We should show the *ton* that Miss Simmons ought to be considered a valued member of society. It is only in keeping her in our company that such a thing can even begin to be considered! Yes, that is what I shall do. I shall ask my friends and those I consider trustworthy to make certain to dance with Miss Simmons and, in that way, we will begin to encourage her back into society."

A slow, dawning light began to grow in Lord Elmsford's face.

"I see. I understand your plan. Initially, I thought that

you alone intended to step out with her, and that, I fear, would have brought a great many questions and whispers with it!"

"No, that is not what I mean," Hugh clarified, quickly. "If I have a few of my friends dance with the lady – and mayhap with the other wallflowers – the *ton* will begin to think a little more highly of her than they do at present. After all, gentlemen will not dance with ladies they think unworthy, will they?"

"Not unless they seek to gain something from them," Lord Elmsford remarked, making Hugh scowl, his smile shattering quickly, "or if they have a connection with them which is a little less than proper."

Hugh rolled his eyes.

"You know very well what I mean! Come now, tell me if that is not a good thought! I think that it is, and I am certain that there will be many who will be willing to sign her dance card."

Looking directly at his friend, he waited until the dawning realization came into Lord Elmsford's eyes.

"You wish me to be the first?"

"Whyever not?"

Lord Elmsford hesitated, a line pulling his brows lower.

"Because I am not certain that I wish to dance."

Hugh's shoulders dropped.

"You do not wish to be spoken about by the *ton*, is that not so?" The lack of response from his friend gave him the answer to his question and, with that, came a flurry of irritation. "My friend, a few moments ago you were congratulating me on saying something to defend

Miss Simmons, even though I knew I ought to have said more, but now, when I have asked you to do something to support the lady, you pull back?"

Shrugging, Lord Elmsford looked away.

"I have had nothing to do with Miss Simmons," he said, as though this was some kind of explanation. "I am only just acquainted with her. When I came to retrieve you and bring you to London, it was so that *your* name might be cleared of the rumors which had begun to assail it. I had no thought nor intention of being of aid to Miss Simmons." With a glance back in Hugh's direction, Lord Elmsford threw up his hands. "And yes, I do not want the *ton* to speak of me, whether it be good or ill. I do not want to be whispered about. In short, I do not want to be *noticed*."

Hugh closed his eyes, the first thrill of excitement beginning to fade as he let Lord Elmsford's words sink in.

"Very well," he muttered, doing his best to understand, rather than let his irritation overpower him. "But all the same, I think the idea is a good one."

"I think it is also. I simply do not want to be the first to step out with her."

The memory of Lady Hastings speaking so cruelly, and the icy looks she had given to Lady Grant sent a whirlwind tearing through Hugh. With a sudden resolve, he lifted his head and looked directly across the room to where Miss Simmons was standing.

"Very well," he declared, his hands curling into tight fists. "If you do not wish to be the first to dance with the lady, then *I* shall be." Without so much as a glance in Lord Elmsford's direction, Hugh walked towards the lady, his determination growing with every step. Whatever dance came next, he would lead Miss Simmons out to the dance floor and, from there, dance with her in full view of all of the other guests.

He only hoped that she would agree.

CHAPTER FOUR

"You spoke with him?"

Rachael grimaced.

"For all the good it did me, yes." With a heavy heart, she shook her head. "I did not intend to speak with him. One moment I was standing talking with you and the next, I found myself beside him."

"And what did you say?" Miss Fairley wanted to know. "What did you say to him?"

Rachael closed her eyes briefly, a little embarrassed.

"I wanted to know if he was going to be doing or saying anything which might be of aid to me, or if he was just going to be concerned with his own standing and nothing more. It was foolish to think that he might be willing to be of aid to me, given that we ought to be doing everything we can to convince the *ton* that there is, and certainly never was, any connection between us."

"But all the same, you were disappointed to hear him say that he cares only for his own situation?"

She nodded, choosing to tell the truth.

"I thought that, on hearing of my situation, he might be willing – nay, eager – to be of aid to me. I thought he might be sorrowful to hear how the *ton* has treated me, even though I have done nothing of what was said and, thereafter, might champion my cause. He, given that he was the other one spoken of, could be best placed to defend me and since he can move about society in a way that I am not, I suppose that I hoped that he might be all the more willing." Her eyes closed briefly. "There was no enthusiasm on his part whatsoever, no real interest or concern. As I have said, it was foolish to let myself hope for that but all the same..."

"All the same, you feel sorrowful over that, I understand." Miss Fairley put a hand on Rachael's arm in a gesture of comfort. "I would very much like to find words to encourage you at this point, but I fear that they would be of very little support to you. All I can say is that I am sorry."

"He is coming over."

Rachael turned to look at Lady Frederica, her brows furrowing.

"I beg your pardon?"

"Lord Blackmore." Lady Frederica was speaking out of the side of her mouth though when she glanced at Rachael, her eyes were suddenly vivid, alive with either surprise or interest. "I do believe that he is making his way towards you!"

With a shake of her head, Rachael did not so much as glance across the ballroom, trying to ignore the knot in her throat.

"Why should he do such a thing as that?"

"Look!" Lady Frederica insisted, forcing Rachael to turn and finally lift her gaze to look in the direction that Lady Frederica was indicating with one hand. It did not take her long to spy Lord Blackmore and, much to her surprise, Lady Frederica appeared to be quite right. He *was* seemingly walking towards her, his gaze fixed on where she stood, and a determination etched across his expression.

She swallowed.

"What could he want with you?"

Miss Fairley came to stand beside Rachael, though she turned her head a little so that it did not appear as though the three of them were simply staring at the gentleman.

"I did see him speaking with some others," Lady Frederica added, her smile growing, though Rachael's did not so much as flicker across her face. "Mayhap something has been said and he wishes now to share it with you."

"Mayhap."

Swallowing quickly, Rachael took a deep breath and then blew it out slowly, feeling the quickening of her heart and aware of the nervousness that ran through her. Lord Blackmore was seemingly very determined indeed, though his progress towards her was slow, given the sheer number of guests whom he had to make his way through. His gaze, however, did not waver and, the nearer he came, the more nervous Rachael grew.

"Here he is!" Miss Fairley whispered though she turned around entirely thereafter, catching Lady Frederica's hand and giving her a small tug so that they could walk a few steps away. "We shall only be a few steps away, Rachael."

Rachael nodded but did not take her eyes from Lord Blackmore. It was more than obvious that his sole intention was to speak with her and, when he was only a short distance away, Rachael dropped to a curtsey, making it plain that she was prepared to speak with him.

"Lord Blackmore?"

He bowed quickly, his face a little flushed.

"Miss Simmons. I wonder if you might dance with me."

Whatever it was that Rachael had been expecting him to say, it had certainly not been this! Her eyes flew wide, and her mouth fell open as her heart began to clamor in her chest.

"Dance with you, Lord Blackmore?"

He nodded.

"Yes."

There was a steeliness to his eyes which she had not seen there before, a strength of purpose which she could not deny. Gone was the gentleman who had not seemed to care about her presence here in London nor the troubles which she suffered on account of the rumors. Instead, he now appeared enthused and resolute.

"You wish to dance with me?" she repeated, seeing him nod. "But Lord Blackmore, given that there have been such rumors about us, do you really think that would be wise?"

He spread out his hands.

"Miss Simmons, I see now what it is that you were suggesting," he said, quietly. "I was in a small group of both ladies and gentlemen and whilst what I have supposedly done can either be explained away or not believed in the least, the different way that they treat *you* is rather shocking, I must admit. I will also say that I attempted to say something – though it was poorly done – and that your good parents did also, but there was not the same response. I confess that I did not see it in the same way when you first spoke to me but now that I have seen it, now I have heard the words coming from their mouths, I find myself to be rather horrified."

"And your solution to this is to dance with me?" Feeling a little overwhelmed, Rachael looked back at him carefully. "Why? What good will it do? Surely it will only start up the rumors again that there is, in fact, a connection between us?"

Lord Blackmore shook his head.

"I think it will do the opposite. It will show the *ton* that we will not let their words affect us, that their whispers are not about to force us into the dark." Seeing her frown, he winced. "You in particular, Miss Simmons."

"But if it is only one dance," she replied, concern beginning to bubble in the pit of her stomach, "then that will certainly make the *ton* talk all the more."

"Oh, it shall not be," Lord Blackmore assured her, quickly. "There will be others. I have made quite certain of that!"

Rachael frowned.

"Oh?"

"I have asked Lord Elmsford to dance with you thereafter, and I intend to have other friends and acquaintances do the same. You see, Miss Simmons, I am now determined to be of aid to you if I can. You are quite right - how the *ton* has treated you in all of this is entirely unfair, and I can see the difficulties it presents now."

Her first instinct was to refuse him, to say that no, she did not – could not – dance with him for fear of what the *ton* would say. This, she held back and considered for a few moments, looking into his face, and seeing the hope glinting in his eyes.

"If you can be assured that other gentlemen will dance with you thereafter, I do not think that there can be any worry in stepping out with Lord Blackmore." Lady Frederica gave her a small smile. "Forgive me for the interruption, but I could not help but overhear, and I understand your concerns, of course." She offered Rachael a small smile but then looked to Lord Blackmore. "Miss Simmons is quite correct to be concerned that, should it only be one dance this evening, one dance with one gentleman, then the *ton* might think all the worse of her for it. What would be better is if your friend might also sign Miss Simmonds' dance card, so that she has the assurance that it will not be only one."

"Of course." Lord Blackmore inclined his head and offered Rachael a small smile, one which sent warmth rippling down her skin. "Do excuse me."

"Good gracious, he is very enthusiastic, is he not?" Rachael looked to Lady Frederica, who only laughed, with Miss Fairley coming to join them also. "I cannot understand it! He states that a single conversation has been enough to force him to change his attitude towards me. That is surprising, I must say!"

"But understandable," Miss Fairley said, with a smile.

"He has only just come back to London, has he not? And I doubt that he would have thought about what impact the rumors would have had on you, for he has been much too busy considering what they mean for *him*. To be present now, to see the other guests treat you differently, compared to how they treat him, is what he has needed to see, to reconsider his position. Perhaps," she continued, gently, "he is a more discerning, more considered gentleman than we first thought him."

"I do not know his character at all well." Rachael kept her gaze on Lord Blackmore for as long as she could, seeing him step through the crowd again in search of his friend. "We were thrown together by this rumor when previously, we had only just been acquainted. I have every desire to stay far from him so that society does not continue with any more rumors – though I am aware that I am the one who went to speak with him first. To dance with him would be quite another thing, however."

"I think you should." Miss Fairley let out a small sigh, then smiled. "It is only a dance. You are already a wall-flower. What else could happen which would make the situation worse?"

Rachael laughed and nodded, albeit rather ruefully.

"I suppose that is true."

"He is returning," Lady Frederica murmured, catching Rachael's hand, and squeezing it. "And with another gentleman beside him."

"Lord Elmsford," Rachael recalled, remembering the gentleman. "He does not look particularly overjoyed at being taken to us."

Lady Frederica snorted.

"I care very little for that. If he asks to dance with you, then you will *have* to agree. It is only right!"

There was no time to say anything more, for Lord Blackmore and Lord Elmsford greeted them and Rachael introduced her friends, noting how Lord Elmsford shifted from foot to foot. Either he was distinctly uncomfortable, or he was entirely uncertain as to what was about to occur.

"You see?" Lord Blackmore gestured to Lord Elmsford with a flourish. "I have found the other gentleman. If you will give him your dance card, then Lord Elmsford will sign it. And if I might have your dance card also, Lady Frederica, Miss Fairley? I am sure that we both can step out with all of you. After all, there are a good few dances remaining." Rachael's heart leaped so high that she was forced to catch her breath, looking back at Lord Blackmore in stunned silence. The other two ladies were just as surprised as she, given that none of them moved and Lord Blackmore frowned, looking from one of them to the next and then back again. "Is there something the matter?"

"You... you wish to dance with all of us?" Rachael breathed, happiness beginning to fill her heart as Lord Blackmore nodded, his confusion evident in his frown. "Are you quite certain?"

"Yes, of course. We both shall." Seeing her bright smile, Lord Blackmore's frown began to lift as he looked back at her. "Does that satisfy you?"

She could not speak for a moment and pulled her dance card from her wrist instead, giving herself time to compose herself.

"Lord Blackmore, Lord Elmsford," she said, softly, "you are both gentlemen of honor, I am sure of it now. Thank you for this kindness."

Lord Elmsford took the dance card from her, smiling now and seemingly a good deal more relaxed than he had been some minutes beforehand.

"But of course," he said, warmly. "Now, let us see which dance I shall take."

∽

"It is our dance, Miss Simmons."

Rachael put one hand to her stomach, nervousness flying through her like a hundred butterflies.

"It is?"

She had been more than a little astonished when Lord Blackmore had written his name down for the waltz, wondering if he had truly meant to do such a thing but when she had queried it, he had simply smiled.

Perhaps there was more to this gentleman than she had first anticipated.

"You look uncertain."

"I am," she admitted, quickly. "It is quite a thing to be standing up with a gentleman to waltz when I have been spending most of this evening hidden in the shadows."

Lord Blackmore smiled and put one hand out to her.

"I understand. But are you ready to dance, Miss Simmons?"

Licking her lips, Rachael pushed aside her nervousness and took his hand, swallowing at the tightness in her throat when he lifted her hand to settle it on his arm.

With a lift of his chin, he walked forward, leading her to the dance floor, and Rachael kept her eyes fixed straight ahead, not allowing herself to look left or right for fear of what – or who – she might see glaring back at her.

"Were you this anxious when you danced with Lord Elmsford?"

Rachael nodded, her stomach now beginning to twist itself this way and that.

"Yes, I was, though I have never before been anxious about dancing the cotillion!"

Lord Blackmore chuckled at this, seemingly quite at ease, his eyes twinkling.

"Then you need have no concern about the waltz, I assure you. We may garner one or two glances, yes, but they can be ignored." The light faded from his eyes as he looked away. "The *ton* should not treat you so disproportionately when both you and I have suffered from attacks by the same rumors. I confess that I did not even think about the impact upon you, not until the moment when I was in conversation with a few others and Lady Hastings spoke so callously, it was difficult to even listen to." Turning his head back to look at her, he smiled quietly. "You asked me if I would do anything to help resolve the situation. I did not realize that there was a need for me to do so, not until after that conversation. I am glad to dance with you now, Miss Simmons. I only hope it will be of help."

"It may be," she murmured, a little surprised at how much her heart had softened towards him, given his actions towards her now. "I thank you, Lord Blackmore. This may be precisely what is needed."

"Let us hope so!"

The music began at the same time as a smile spread across his face and, before she knew it, Rachael found herself caught up in his arms. One hand was in hers, the other settled at her waist, and his guiding steps were leading her in the waltz as they danced across the ballroom floor. Rachael's heart grew a little faster, worried about what those watching might think, worried about what they might say, her gaze darting all around the ballroom.

"Do not look at them." Her eyes went to Lord Blackmore's face. The smile that had settled there still remained, though it was gentle now, his eyes searching hers. "You are still anxious," he continued, his steps every sure as they danced together. "I can feel the tension in your frame. Look only at me, Miss Simmons. Do your best to forget those around you."

Rachael forced her eyes to settle on his, her heart clamoring still but, as she gazed up at him, the tension which had bound itself to her limbs began to dissipate. Slowly, she began to enjoy the dance, finding herself a little lost in Lord Blackmore's eyes.

"That is better now," he murmured, his soft words only a little louder than the music, seeming to twine in between the notes as he smiled down at her. "You are simply a young lady of society dancing with a gentleman of society. That is all."

Rachael pressed her lips tightly together, aware that there was something new taking the place of the tension that had bound itself to her. It was not a strain nor an ache, however, but a sweet warmth that made her smile, her steps a little lighter now, and her happiness growing with every moment. This was the first time that she had stepped out with a gentleman since the rumors had begun to circulate last Season. Of course, no gentleman of repute had wanted to dance with her once they believed that she was either betrothed to Lord Blackmore because of their connection *or* because she was a lady with no moral character. It was strange now to be dancing in the very gentleman's arms whom the *ton* believed she had a prior connection with – but no, she would not consider that at the present moment. Lord Blackmore was quite right, she should enjoy this rather than grow anxious over it.

All too soon, the music came to an end and, with a soft sigh, Rachael curtsied to Lord Blackmore.

"Thank you. I enjoyed that very much."

"You mean, you began to enjoy it the moment you let go of the tension and worry you held within yourself." Bowing low, he offered her his arm. "Let me walk you back to your friends."

Rachael smiled and took his arm, noting first the delighted smile of her mother, who had seen them dancing. There was a happiness there, a glistening in her eyes that spoke of genuine relief and joy – the very same that Rachael was feeling within her heart.

That feeling began to fade at the same moment that Lord Elmsford strode forward, making his way to Lord Blackmore's side.

"Forgive me," he murmured, as Rachael looked on, wondering what had taken place that concerned the gentleman so much that he had come out to meet Lord Blackmore. "Blackmore, I must speak with you."

"What is the matter?" Lord Blackmore continued walking, though his steps were a little slower now. "Is there something wrong?"

Lord Elmsford's eyes darted towards Rachael, and she stiffened, the familiar tension now clawing back through her.

"Pray, if it concerns me, then you must not be afraid to tell me of it."

"It does not concern you, Miss Simmons, though you might wish to be careful of spending more time in Lord Blackmore's company," he replied, making Rachael's eyebrows lift. "There is another rumor being spread, I am afraid, and this time, it only concerns you, Blackmore."

Her heart slammed hard against her ribs as she quickly pulled her arm away from Lord Blackmore's, wanting the happy moment she had shared with him to linger, though it was already cracking into tiny pieces and being blown away by the wind.

"Another rumor? It cannot be true, given that you have only just returned to London!"

"Of course it is not true," Lord Blackmore returned, his eyes sharp, but his upset clearly directed towards this news. "What is it then, Elmsford? What is it that you have heard?"

Lord Elmsford once more looked to Rachael, but she remained where she was, wanting to hear what had been said and, since Lord Blackmore did not object, Lord Elmsford continued quickly.

"I have only heard it this evening, and I do not know

why it has come about, nor who has said such a thing. It seems very strange indeed that it should come about now but–"

"What is being said, Elmsford?"

The gentleman's hard tone made Rachael's eyes flare, though Lord Elmsford only sighed.

"It is that you are deep in debt to the Red Fox – the gambling den on the west side of London," he said, as Rachael caught her breath. "And that you are now without hope and must marry a lady with an excellent dowry... no matter who she may be."

Rachael closed her eyes.

"Which means that whispers will soon begin that *I* am the one you might settle on," she murmured, opening her eyes to see Lord Elmsford nodding. "Goodness. We have already been battling some very difficult rumors and yet more assail us? Why?"

Lord Blackmore pinched the bridge of his nose and shook his head, his eyes settling on hers though they held no flickering hope, no spark of determination. Instead, they were a dull, dark green and, as his shoulders dropped, Rachael's spirits went with them.

"I do not know," he answered, his voice low. "It seems as though my return to London has brought more difficulties than I ever expected."

CHAPTER FIVE

"Good afternoon."

Hugh grimaced as the two gentlemen walked into his study.

"You are sure that you wish to call on me, Lord Kelling? Has not Lord Elmsford told you about the circulating rumors?"

"He has but, of course, I do not believe them," Lord Kelling replied, with a grin. "I came to see if I could be of any assistance to you."

"Assistance?" Hugh gestured for both men to sit down. "I am afraid that I do not know what can be done! I am supposedly greatly in debt to one of the worst gambling dens in all of London and, therefore, the *ton* now believes that I have very little coin and cannot be at all financially secure."

Lord Kelling shrugged.

"Given that you have not been in London for more than a sennight, I find that very difficult to believe."

"Precisely!" Lord Elmsford sat down in one of the comfortable chairs and shrugged. "I am sure that there will be others in the *ton* who will realize that."

"Though that does not aid me at present," Hugh remarked, with a small sigh. "I have just now finished writing to my brother, telling him that it would not be wise to come to London. Initially, I told him the same, only to write again and state that I was coming to London after all. Now, however, I continue to advise him to remain in Bath."

Lord Kelling nodded.

"A considerate thought," he agreed, quietly. "And how is your brother? Is he as much of an oaf as he always was?"

This brought a smile to Hugh's face, despite his inner frustrations.

"Yes, I am afraid that Alderton is just as foolish as he has always been. Did I tell you that he married last year?"

Lord Kelling's eyes widened.

"No, you did not!"

Hugh shrugged his shoulders.

"I only knew of it after it had taken place, thanks to a letter the lady herself sent me rather than my own brother informing me of it. I have not even met Lady Alderton as yet! My father despaired of him and, I confess, I do the same. Quite what he is doing in Bath rather than at his own estate with his wife – though she might well be with him – I do not know." With their mother having passed away many years ago and their father shortly thereafter, Hugh had always been the one to take on responsibilities and the like, given that he had become the new Earl of Blackmore, whilst Porter – now the Viscount Alderton – was the one eager to spend as much money as he wished. With their father's will dividing things between them, Hugh had decided many years ago to leave his brother to do as he pleased with not only his own money but his own, smaller, estate. Thus far, it had suited him very well to forget all about what Alderton was doing. He had his own concerns and none of them were about what his brother might be involved with at any given moment. The only reason he knew Alderton was in Bath at present was that his brother had deigned to write to him and inform him of such a thing, though he had not mentioned whether his wife was with him or not.

"It is probably better for you that he does not come to London." With a wry smile, Lord Kelling glanced to Lord Elmsford, who nodded fervently. "All the same, it is rather troubling that this rumor has risen– seemingly from nowhere!"

"And during the time that I was dancing with Miss Simmons," Hugh added with a scowl. "That will have affected her too and that is frustrating indeed." Lord Elmsford and Lord Kelling exchanged a look and Hugh narrowed his eyes, seeing that there was something between them that was not yet spoken. "What is it?"

"It is as I thought," Lord Elmsford said, with a shake of his head. "The *ton* have begun to suggest that you will betroth yourself to Miss Simmons, given that you were dancing with her last evening. Because they think you without coin, then it is said that no young lady would consent to marry you, knowing that you seek only their dowry, and whatever fortune they might bring. However, someone like Miss Simmons, someone without any opportunity to marry, given what is said of *her,* will accept you. And though her father is only a Viscount and you an Earl, Lord Grant is not without fortune!"

Closing his eyes, Hugh's jaw clenched tightly, fire igniting in his belly. Miss Simmons was someone who had already been injured – severely so – by a rumor relating both to him and to her, though she had never once done anything akin to what had been said of her. Last evening, he had determined to do whatever he could to aid her and assist her back into good standing in society, but now, with this rumor adding to the heavyweight already settling on her, she would be more affected than ever before.

"It is unfortunate."

"Who would do such a thing?" Throwing up his hands, Hugh then pushed himself out of his chair and walked directly across the room to where his whisky sat. Pouring a measure into three glasses, he handed one to each of his friends before picking up the third for himself. "I do not understand why someone would make up a rumor in that regard. Why would they speak ill of me? Why would they try to make society think all the more poorly of me? As you have said, Lord Kelling, I am only just returned to London and now, it seems, I am to suffer yet further disgrace. There is no way to prove such a thing, not unless I go to the gambling den, find the proprietor, and haul him to a soiree or the like, where he might declare that I am not at all in debt to either himself or any other establishments that he might know of." With a roll of his eyes, he took a sip of his whisky. "Though I might very well not be invited to any further soirees or balls, not when I have already been so disgraced."

"Then you must have your own!" Lord Kelling sat forward in his chair, excitement in his eyes now. "Indeed, would that not solve a great many difficulties? You would be able to show the *ton* that you are not without coin, as they believe, and you might then be able to assure the guests that such a rumor is nothing but nonsense. Your friends will be able to confirm it, I am sure!"

Lord Elmsford nodded, a smile splitting his features as, for the first time, hope began to build in Hugh's chest.

"I may be able to do such a thing," he said, slowly, as Lord Elmsford grinned. "It would have to be a magnificent ball."

"With no expense spared, "Lord Kelling agreed, as Hugh began to nod, his heart slowly lifting free of the worries and concerns which had held it for the last few hours. "It will prove to society that you have more than enough money, for what gentleman would spend money on a ball when he had none?"

Hugh threw back the rest of his whisky and slammed it down on the desk before grinning back at his friends. "Precisely! I think that a capital idea, Lord Kelling!"

"It is an expensive idea."

Laughing at Lord Elmsford's remark, Hugh shrugged his shoulders.

"I have not spent any money this Season as yet. I was always going to have to do something, whether it be a soiree, dinner, or a ball. And as Lord Kelling said, a ball is just the occasion I need to prove that this rumor is false."

"Very well. Then a ball it is!" Lord Elmsford grinned and lifted his glass. "And I do hope that you will serve some of your very fine French brandy rather than this whisky – although it is also very good."

Hugh chuckled and, for the first time since his friends had arrived, felt himself in a rather positive frame of mind. Already he was thinking about what would come next, what would happen, and what society's reaction would be. Surely they would no longer be able to even *think* that what was being said of him was true!

"Are you going to do anything to find out who it is that is speaking about you in such a way?"

Lord Kelling's question had Hugh's smile shattering.

"You mean, the person who began this rumor about me?"

Lord Kelling nodded.

"Might it be the same person who spoke ill of you before?

At this, Hugh quickly shook his head.

"No, I do not think it could be. Last Season, it was simply a case of mistaken identity. Someone must have seen Miss Simmons – or someone who looked like Miss Simmons – coming out of a townhouse. They mistakenly believed that it was *my* townhouse when it was not. Thus, my name was pulled in towards that of Miss Simmons and as such, the rumors began."

"Then you do not think there could be any connection?"

Hugh shook his head no to Lord Elmsford's question.

"I would doubt it."

"Which begs the question what are you going to do?" With a look to Lord Kelling, Lord Elmsford rose to his feet and went to pour another measure of whisky. "Are you going to find out who is responsible?"

"I would not know how to go about that."

"It is simple enough, though it might take some time. All you would need to do would be to ask each person in turn who they heard the story from, beginning with Lord Elmsford," Lord Kelling explained. "Lord Elmsford?"

"I overheard it rather than being told directly," Lord Elmsford said, sitting down again, his glass of whisky refilled. "I heard Lord Gallagher and Lady Yateley speaking together of it."

"And was it Lady Yateley telling Lord Gallagher, or the other way around?"

"The other way around. It was certainly Lord Gallagher telling Lady Yateley the news, for she appeared greatly astonished."

"Then that gives us something we can do," Lord Kelling said, flinging a triumphant look to Hugh. "You will need to ask Lord Gallagher where he heard this rumor from."

"Or I can do so," Lord Elmsford suggested. "That way, he might be more willing to speak with me rather than telling someone who the rumor is about!"

"That is true enough, I suppose." Hugh gestured towards Lord Elmsford. "Well, if you are willing to do such a thing, I would be grateful."

Lord Elmsford nodded.

"But of course." A hint of a smile brushed at his lips. "And tell me, what of Miss Simmons?"

A little confused at Lord Elmsford's tone, Hugh frowned.

"What do you mean, what of her?"

"Was she pleased to be dancing with you? She did not say much to me."

Hugh looked down at his whisky glass.

"I think she was, in the end." Recalling how tight her expression had been, how her eyes had darted from one side of the room to the other, he shook his head. "She was very anxious initially. At the end of the dance, however, she was a good deal happier." His smile grew gently, glad that she had managed to relax a little and lose some of her anxiety. "I believe that it was the first dance she had stepped out to – save for yours, Elmsford – since she had first heard that rumor spreading across London."

"I am glad to hear it. I have wondered if…" With a shake of his head, Lord Elmsford dropped his gaze to his whisky glass. "It does not matter."

A little confused as to what it was Lord Elmsford had been going to say, and why he had stopped himself, Hugh opened his mouth to ask him to explain, only for Lord Kelling to interrupt.

"I did not manage to dance with the lady myself, but I have every intention of doing so at the next ball," he promised, as Hugh smiled his agreement. "You are quite right, the wallflowers ought not to be ignored if there is nothing that *they* have done that deserves being ignored. I promise I shall stand up with Miss Simmons at the next ball we both attend. Perhaps I shall converse with her thereafter for Lord Elmsford has stated that she is rather beautiful."

Hugh's eyebrows lifted high as Lord Elmsford snorted and rolled his eyes.

"I mentioned that she was pretty, I think. I am sure you would not disagree, Blackmore?"

Considering, Hugh brought Miss Simmons' expression to mind – and found himself immediately lost in the memory of how she had smiled up into his eyes during their waltz. There had been a gentleness there, a joy which had infused every part of her expression and it had altered her appearance so drastically that he had been quite taken with her. Had there not been any difficulties between them and society, had there not been the rumors and the whispers, then Hugh might have decided to consider her and called to take tea – but at present, the only thing he wanted to think about was making sure that society did not believe any of the rumors which surrounded him.

And perhaps I also wish to think about the question of who is so determined to ruin my reputation that they would spread such lies.

"You were beginning to consider matrimony, were you not?"

Lord Kelling's question had Hugh's eyebrows lifting.

"I beg your pardon?"

"Last Season," his friend said, with a grin. "Did you not begin to think on matrimony? That you would find the right young lady and court her and the like?"

Hugh waved a hand.

"I considered that last Season, only for that rumor to

put an end to such thoughts! I cannot permit myself to think on that again, not until I am certain that the *ton* thinks of me in the way they ought."

Lord Kelling considered this for a moment, then nodded.

"Very well. Though if Miss Simmons is –"

"Miss Simmons needs to regain her standing in much the same way as I do," Hugh interrupted, quickly, finding that he did not want his friends to make such a suggestion, even though he had noticed a little interest in his own heart when he had been dancing with her. "Come now, that is not the concern at present! Surely you can both see that?"

"Are you going to invite Miss Simmons and her parents to the ball?" Lord Elmsford asked, pointedly. "Is she going to have one of your invitations?"

"Of course she shall." Hugh did not let his friends' smiles, or the looks they sent to each other, embarrass him in the least. "But I intend to invite all of them – all of the wallflowers, that is – as well as many others. I will not exclude them."

"Then I applaud you in that," Lord Elmsford replied, as Hugh rose to his feet and made his way across to his desk. "If we can be of help to you then please do ask."

"You can be of help to me," Hugh replied, immediately, throwing a grin across to his friend. "You can aid me by stating who I ought to invite. That will be of the biggest assistance."

Thankfully, Lord Kelling and Lord Elmsford both seemed eager to help and, within the hour, Hugh not only had a guest list, but also suggestions of all that he might want to do at the ball, all that might prove to the guests that he had more than enough coin to do whatever he pleased. Surely that would be proof enough?

∽

"Good afternoon, Lady Grant. Good afternoon, Miss Simmons." Hugh smiled as warmly as he could and inclined his head. "How good to see you again, Miss Simmons. I do hope that you are quite well?"

They paused in their walk down the London street, and Miss Simmons smiled, but it did not send a single flicker of light into her eyes. Her face was rather pale, and her shoulders a little hunched. Evidently, the *ton*'s treatment of her was still causing a great deal of difficulty for her. Frustration ran through Hugh's thoughts, and he frowned hard.

"We are all well, I thank you."

Lady Grant offered him a small smile, but her glance towards her daughter said more than she had spoken aloud. There was something that had upset Miss Simmons, but her mother, and the lady herself, were both unwilling to disclose it.

His stomach dropped. *Is this because of me?*

"I should like to inform you that I plan to throw a magnificent ball," he said, wondering if this would bring a smile to Miss Simmons' face. "I will make certain to invite all of you– and your friends also, Miss Simmons."

Her blue eyes turned to his and a wave of heat ran from the top of his head all the way down to his toes as he took her in. She was pretty, as Lord Elmsford had said, but, as Hugh studied her, he silently considered that he would describe her in stronger terms, rather than as merely pretty. Her dark curls danced lightly about her forehead, her alabaster skin, with the gentle pink of her lips and blue eyes were the very essence of beauty. He only wished that she would smile.

"You are very kind to be so considerate, Lord Blackmore," she said, though she still did not smile. "I am not certain, however, that it would be wise for me to attend. I may bring more disruption with me, and you do not require that, I am sure."

Hugh took a step closer, instinctive in his desire to reassure her.

"Not at all, Miss Simmons. I would very much like you to be present. Indeed, it is one of my strongest desires. You asked me if I would be of aid to you if I would help you in regaining your standing within society, and I genuinely wish to do so. I hope that I have imparted that to you already."

"You have, and I am truly appreciative of such a desire," came the reply, as Lady Grant tactfully stepped away, going to speak to another acquaintance who, much to Hugh's relief, seemed quite contented to speak with her. "But I fear that... well, in truth, Lord Blackmore, it seems that society is determined to attach rumors to both of us and, as it has been pointed out to me, if I had not stood up with you to dance, then the rumor about our potential betrothal due to your lack of funds might never have begun."

Hugh frowned.

"That is not something which ought to have been

said to you, Miss Simmons. This rumor is about me and my supposed lack of funds. Why you have been attached to that is quite beyond me – and I believe that it would have come about whether or not we stepped out to dance together. It seems to me that someone is willing to do whatever they can to injure me, in ways that I had not expected, and, in doing so, they have pulled your name into it also. I can only apologize for that, and reassure you that I am doing my utmost to prove that this story about my being in debt is utterly untrue."

Her eyes searched his, her lips twisting as she considered what he had said. A long, heavy breath came from her as she dropped her head, shaking it gently as though she was uncertain as to how she ought to respond.

"Might I ask who said such a thing to you?"

Miss Simmons lifted her head and looked back at him.

"Lady Tabitha."

Hugh's eyebrows lifted.

"Lady Hastings' daughter?"

"The very same."

Hugh shook his head.

"Lady Hastings was one of the harshest creatures I spoke with of late. She is unbending, unflinching, and unyielding. It does not surprise me that her daughter is the same. If I were you, Miss Simmons, I would do your utmost to ignore the lady's words. There is no kindness there."

Miss Simmons laughed softly, though there was still a light sheen in her eyes.

"That is wise advice, Lord Blackmore. I shall do as you ask."

"Very good." His own smile grew. "And will you come to my ball? Will you promise me to attend? If you do, I can assure you that you will have more than one gentleman asking you to dance."

Miss Simmons looked back at him for some seconds then, with a quick smile, nodded.

"Very well, Lord Blackmore. I shall make certain to attend."

"Capital! And I shall make certain to dance with you," he promised, finding his heart suddenly alive with anticipation and happiness over the thought of her joining him at the ball. "In truth, I am very glad indeed that you have chosen to come, Miss Simmons. These rumors might very well be difficult to bear, but it is important that we do our utmost to stand against them. We must not let them crush us, must not permit them to overwhelm us. If we do, then we will let the darkness catch us up in its arms and it will be very difficult indeed to free ourselves from it again."

It took a few seconds for Miss Simmons to respond but, when she did, it was with a steady gaze, a quiet nod and only a hint of a smile on her lips. Hugh found himself reaching out, one hand going to hers and, as he took it, the shock which widened her eyes filtered through to his own heart also. What exactly was he doing?

Clearing his throat, Hugh bowed over Miss Simmons' hand but did not release it once he had lifted his head. Instead, he held it in his own, ignoring the fact that they were standing in the middle of a London street and, instead, focusing on the pain in her eyes.

"I understand that you have a good deal more difficulty than I," he said, quietly. "I speak of darkness and of standing against it, I speak of difficulties and struggle, only to remind myself that you have already a greater battle to fight than I. To be pressed back into the shadows, to have the *ton* consider you a wallflower must be a great trial. And," he continued, eventually releasing her hand, "it must be all the more difficult, seeing that I can walk about society just as I please and without anything to hold me back."

Again, she let out a quiet laugh, but this one was filled with a harshness that Hugh recognized to be pain. His heart swelled and he stepped closer, only for Lady Grant to come to join them.

"Forgive me for stepping away," she said, as Hugh cleared his throat and moved back just a little, quietly wondering to himself what it was that he had been intending to do when it came to Miss Simmons.

Had he thought to grasp her hand again? To speak all the more fervently? Why did his arms ache, his heart clasp tight in pain? Was it because he had wanted to pull her close, to hold her in his arms in a vague attempt to soothe her pain?

A heat began to build in his chest as he inclined his head.

"But of course, Lady Grant. Miss Simmons and I have just been speaking about my upcoming ball."

"Oh?"

Seeing the way Lady Grant's gaze slid towards her

daughter, the worry etched across her forehead, Hugh smiled quickly.

"Miss Simmons has agreed to attend, which I am delighted about. I will have the invitations sent out by the end of this week and will make certain that what I have promised, Miss Simmons, will be set in place also." With a smile, he bowed and, upon lifting his head, saw the flicker that ran across Miss Simmons' lips. It was not a smile of warmth, nor happiness, but one of uncertainty. Hugh's heart turned over on itself, silently praying that she was not about to change her mind and refuse to attend his ball. For whatever reason – a reason that Hugh did not wish to consider at that moment – her presence at the ball was swiftly becoming very important to him.

"I shall take my leave now," he murmured, bowing to Lady Grant. "It was very pleasant to speak with you both and, please, do look out for my invitation."

"We shall." Lady Grant spoke fervently and with a good deal of warmth in her tone as she smiled. "Thank you, Lord Blackmore."

"Thank you." Miss Simmons looked back into his eyes, and Hugh's breath quickened a fraction, simply from the action of holding her gaze with his. "You have been very encouraging, Lord Blackmore."

He put one hand to his heart, finding it difficult to step away from her.

"I will do what I can, Miss Simmons," he promised. "These rumors will pass, and we shall both be free to take our place in society again, I can assure you."

With that, he forced himself to turn and walk away, wondering silently why his heart was beginning to fill with a determination to return to her side already. Yes, she was beautiful and yes, he found himself sympathetic and even a little guilty for what she was enduring at present – but was there something more there? And if there was, then what precisely was he meant to do about it?

CHAPTER SIX

"It is good to be recognized, at least."

Rachael smiled at Miss Bosworth, one of the newest wallflowers who was now standing by Lady Alice. It had been a month since her return to London and their little band of wallflowers now numbered five.

"Though to be recognized for the wrong reasons is hardly fair."

"Indeed." Miss Bosworth sighed, shaking her head. "I am glad that we have all decided that to push ourselves forward into society is something we ought to do, however. I have no desire to stand back, to let the shadows reduce me to nothing but a blur of black and grey and to have society ignore my presence."

Rachael considered this, and then found herself nodding.

"I must admit that I agree wholeheartedly. It is very difficult to maintain, however, is it not? I have found this last sennight that I have garnered nothing but dark looks, with lips curling and eyes narrowing."

Lady Alice smiled ruefully.

"I will admit to that also, though I have done my best to ignore it. If society is to see us as we are, then we must force our presence upon them. It is clear that they do not much like it, however!"

"I care very little as to whether or not they like it," Lady Frederica declared, with a toss of her head. "We have friends here. They may be few in number, but we do have them! There are a few gentlemen, and one or two ladies who will acknowledge us. The gentlemen who dance with us seem to me to be the very best sort of gentlemen." Tilting her head, Rachael looked back at Lady Frederica who, seeing her look, laughed and shook her head. "No, I am not about to fall in love with any of them, if that is your question," she said, as Rachael smiled at her. "I know all too well that, whilst a gentleman might be kind, he will not have any intention of marrying a wallflower. To take tea with one of us would be shocking enough!"

"I suppose that is true." Rachael smiled to herself as she remembered how Lord Blackmore had spoken to her so kindly the previous week, how he had taken her hand and held it tightly for a few moments. It had been a gesture of comfort, of encouragement, she was sure, but all the same, there had been a warmth in her heart which had caught her unawares. When she had looked into his eyes, when she had seen the gentleness in his expression and heard him speak so softly to her, she had felt her heart quicken. It was the first time that a gentleman had ever shown any sort of interest in her but, as she had reminded herself furiously, Lord Blackmore was doing it all simply to be kind. Evidently, seeing how differently she was being treated by the *ton* in comparison to him had been enough for him to take action, to truly feel for her and thus, that was what he was doing. The reason for his ball was, of course, to quash the rumor that he had no coin whatsoever – something that was already beginning to take place now that invitations had gone out – and his desire to not only invite her to join him, but also to dance with her, came from an eagerness to be of aid to her as she battled the whispers which still clung to her. There was nothing more than that to his desire, she was sure, and yet her thoughts continually threatened to pull in a different direction altogether.

"Though it is good of Lord Blackmore to invite us all to his ball."

Hearing his name, Rachael jumped slightly as she came back to the conversation, having been lost in her own thoughts on that very gentleman.

"Yes, it is."

"Though it is a shame that there are still such rumors about him," Miss Fairley sighed. "There are still those who believe that he is entirely without coin, that this ball is nothing more than a sham."

Rachael laughed and shook her head.

"Do they expect to turn up to his townhouse and see nothing there? The house empty, the ballroom dark and Lord Blackmore to be entirely absent?"

"Mayhap." Miss Fairley chuckled quietly. "It is a foolish thing to believe, I know. Though I do not understand why someone would begin that rumor about him in the first place."

"Nor do I," Rachael agreed, a frown replacing her smile as she considered. Though she herself was caught up in the rumor, Rachael had been wondering why yet another piece of gossip had been started about Lord Blackmore. From what she knew, he was a fine, upstanding gentleman and yet this was now the second rumor which had been about him. "It is as though someone is determined to demean him, to ruin his character in the eyes of the *ton*, though I cannot imagine why."

"Nor I." With a slight lift of her shoulders, Lady Frederica turned her head to look at the many guests behind them. "Who can understand why the *ton* act in the way that they do? Mayhap someone simply found enjoyment in preparing a particular bit of gossip and chose Lord Blackmore merely because they could."

Rachael's stomach twisted, her heart sinking.

"Mayhap. It seems a great shame to try to ruin a gentleman's reputation for the sake of a little entertainment."

"And your own reputation also," her friend reminded her, as the other wallflowers nodded. "You have not had any more encounters with Lady Tabitha, I hope?"

Wincing, Rachael recalled the moment when she had made to step into a bookshop, only for Lady Tabitha to step out first. The scathing look which had been sent in Rachael's direction had gone directly to her heart, but she had forced herself not to respond to it by letting her expression change. Instead, she had lifted her chin, looking back into Lady Tabitha's hazel eyes, and had bid her a hearty, 'good afternoon'.

That had been a mistake. What had followed had been a tirade of sharp words which had thrown themselves at Rachael and brought her a great deal of pain. It had centered solely on how Rachael ought not to be present in London, how she should have remained back at her father's estate and found a simple gentleman to marry, rather than returning to face her shame here. Rachael had found enough strength to protest, to state quite clearly that she had done nothing wrong and to suggest, boldly, that those who believed such rumors were rather foolish. This had brought yet more stinging condescension with it, though Rachael had chosen not to stand and allow the lady's tirade to continue. Instead, she had spoken a loud, 'good day, Lady Tabitha' and had walked into the bookshop, leaving her mother to follow her. Once inside, she had dissolved into tears, though her mother had done her best to comfort her, assuring her that she had spoken well, and done nothing wrong.

It had not lessened the pain.

"I have not spoken with her since that day," she said, as Lady Frederica scowled, clearly recalling what Rachael had told them about what had taken place. "And I have no intention of doing so either, though I cannot say what Lady Tabitha's intentions are! Mayhap she intends to come and find me and throw yet more upon my head!"

"Then you would wish to know if she were to approach?" Lady Alice's gaze narrowed, and Rachael made to look over her shoulder, only for Lady Alice to shake her head no. "She is present. I can see her looking over at us, though she has not taken a step closer to us as yet."

Rachael sighed.

"I shall take a short turn about the ballroom, I think," she said, aware of the knot in her stomach. "I do not want Lady Tabitha to come to speak with us for, no doubt, she will cause you all the same pain that she caused me. No doubt she is displeased with the audacity with which I spoke to her of late, and I would not be surprised if she were to go on to say something – either true or untrue – which might very well make the *ton* think all the more ill of us!" With a quick smile, she stepped away. "I will return shortly."

Her parents had become used to allowing Rachael the freedom to stand with the other wallflowers while they made their way around the ballroom and, even though it was not proper for her to be walking in the ballroom without a chaperone, Rachael did not care. No-one would look at her. She was, as she had come to realize, almost entirely invisible to the *ton* and anyone who so much as glanced at her would not look back at her again, or wonder who she was. Her presence would barely be acknowledged.

Walking slowly, her hands clasped loosely in front of her, Rachael found herself thinking on Lord Blackmore again. His kindness was not something she had expected, especially given how she had been forced to *ask* for his consideration at first! Now, however, he appeared to be determined to do what he could to help her and, for that, Rachael was more than grateful.

I only wish my heart would not quicken so whenever he should look at me.

Coming to a set of double doors – one of which was

held open by a hook and a latch – and the other closed, Rachael glanced through it into the hallway, merely from idle curiosity, only to see something which caused her to stand quite still.

Lord Blackmore?

The gentleman was laughing at something another gentleman was saying, with three of them standing together in the hallway. She did not know what it was that he was saying, nor what was so mirthful but, all the same, the smile on his face and the light in his eyes made her smile.

"They are there?"

Rachael blinked, turning her head to see two figures standing a short distance from her. She could not make out their faces and, no doubt, they were not easily able to see her, given the darkness of this part of the room. All the same, she stepped away at once, moving back along the wall and, seeing a vacant chair, sat down in it carefully. The last thing she needed at this moment was for anyone to notice her and, thereafter, exclaim over her lack of propriety in walking through the ballroom alone.

"What do you plan to do?"

"What we have been asked to do," the other voice said, as Rachael turned her head away, hoping such a gesture showed a lack of interest, should either of the two gentlemen realize she was there. "We must find a way to start some gossip about Lord Blackmore. If he is in there with his friends, then why do we not send... Lady Duthell to him?"

Rachael's breath caught in her chest as she stared straight ahead, not looking back to where the two gentlemen stood, but straining to hear what was to be said next. They were speaking of Lord Blackmore, of wanting to encourage gossip, to have yet more whispers surround him? Why?

"Do you think Lady Duthell will do as we ask?"

The second man chuckled, sending a dark chill down Rachael's spine.

"Lady Duthell will go where we tell her, especially if we state that there is an eager and willing gentleman waiting for her."

Rachael closed her eyes and tried to breathe steadily, unable to move from where she was but, at the same time, desperate to see who these gentlemen were, to see their faces so that she might help Lord Blackmore identify them should it come to it. Slowly, she turned her head, squinting as she tried to make out their faces, but neither gentleman was identifiable. The shadows were too great. All she could see was that one was taller than the other, but both were standing close together, their low tones barely loud enough for her to hear over the music and buzz of conversation.

"He has friends there," the first complained. "We cannot have Lady Duthell sent to him if his friends are present. How–"

"We will have one of the staff do our bidding," the second interrupted, sounding a little frustrated now. "Go. Tell Lady Duthell that she must make her way to the parlor. Tell her that a gentleman is waiting to speak with her." A quiet chuckle had Rachael's eyes squeezing closed. "I can promise you that she will go there at once."

"And for Lord Blackwell?

"A footman will tell him that Lord Kelling requires his help and is waiting for him in the parlor," the second said, clearly the one who was able to organize matters without so much as a thought. "I do wonder if you have anything to contribute in this matter, given that you are so cloth-headed!"

Rachael swallowed hard, her fingers locking together as she watched the two gentlemen separate. She rose swiftly, her legs a little unsteady as she stepped forward, trying to spy one of them, trying to see their faces, but they had already disappeared into the crowd of guests.

I must warn Lord Blackmore.

Her breath catching in her chest, Rachael hurried back to the door and, stepping through it, came face to face with Lord Blackmore. His smile grew a little fixed, the laughter in his eyes starting to fade the moment he laid eyes on her.

"Miss... Simmons." Speaking slowly, Lord Blackmore gazed to the open door, clearly wondering if he was about to see a chaperone of some sort coming after her. "You are alone?"

"Lord Blackmore," Rachael began, barely glancing at the other two gentlemen, "I have just now overheard something most grievous, and I have come to warn you of it."

The remaining lightness in Lord Blackmore's face disappeared completely.

"What is it, Miss Simmons?"

"Two gentlemen spied you in here," she said, aware of just how breathless she was, how much tension was humming through her. "I do not know who they were, I did not hear their titles and, try as I might, I could not see their faces. There were too many shadows clinging to the back of the room – but oh, Lord Blackmore, you *must* be careful!"

Lord Blackmore moved closer to her at once, his hand finding hers though her blue eyes were suddenly a little darker as he searched her expression.

"What have you overheard, Miss Simmons? Please, do tell us at once. I can see that you are distressed by it."

Rachael swallowed quickly and began her explanation.

"Two gentlemen are conspiring to bring yet more gossip to shame you," she began, her heart thudding painfully. "One is to go to a footman who will then come to tell you that Lord Kelling is waiting for you in the parlor, and asks that you go to him at once."

"Lord Kelling?" Lord Blackmore glanced behind him. "I have Lord Elmsford present here and Lord Richmond also, but Lord Kelling is somewhere in the ballroom. Why would he wish to see me in the parlor?"

"It will not be Lord Kelling waiting for you there," Rachael explained, her face heating as she looked away from Lord Blackmore. "It will be... a lady."

There was nothing but silence for a few moments and, as Rachael slowly returned her eyes to his face, she saw the scarlet dots begin to appear in his cheeks. Lord Elmsford and Lord Richmond both turned to look at Lord Blackmore also and seeing what it was that they thought, Rachael hurried to explain.

"It is not a lady that you yourself will have asked to meet," she said, hastily, "but rather one that these two gentlemen will have sent there to meet you. A Lady Duthell?"

Lord Richmond's exclamation came at once.

"Lady Duthell? She is a widow known for her... interest in as many connections with as many different gentlemen as she can!" Rachael closed her eyes as fire burned up through her chest and into her face. "Forgive me," Lord Richmond said, immediately, clearly aware that he had embarrassed her by speaking so openly. "But yes, I can now understand what you mean, Miss Simmons. Someone intends to have Lord Blackmore seen in the company of Lady Duthell—"

"And in a private parlor, no less," Lord Elmsford added, a frown darkening his forehead. "That is a little concerning, I must say."

"No doubt someone will then come along and open that door – or be placed in a position where they can see only you and Lady Duthell emerging," Rachael finished, biting her lip when Lord Blackmore scowled. "I do not know who would do such a thing, or why. I am only glad that I have been able to inform you of it all."

Lord Blackmore let out a heavy sigh.

"As am I." His sharp eyes caught hers. "And you say you do not know their names? You did not see their faces?"

Rachael shook her head.

"I did not. Would that I had."

"Do not feel any guilt whatsoever, I beg of you." Despite the tension which now ran through them all, Lord Blackmore smiled and, reaching out, caught her hand for a moment, his fingers warm on hers. "You have saved me from a great and terrible trial! I am grateful to you."

She nodded, letting out a slow breath which stole some of her worry from her.

"I only wish that I could have done more. I—"

Behind her, the door opened, and Lord Blackmore dropped her hand at once, leaving her with a sudden sense of loss.

"Forgive me, my Lords." The footman bowed, but kept his gaze low. "I believe that one of you is Lord Blackmore?"

Rachael turned, looking with wide eyes up to Lord Blackmore, all the more astonished when he nodded.

"My Lord, I have a message for you from Lord Kelling. He is in urgent need of your help and asks you to make your way to the parlor."

"The parlor?" Lord Blackmore repeated, as the footman nodded. "Might I ask who gave you this message?"

The footman blinked.

"It was from Lord Kelling, my Lord."

"*He* was the one who told you to find me here?"

With no pause nor hesitation whatsoever, the footman nodded.

"Yes, Lord Blackmore. He came to me only a few minutes ago, stated who he was and instructed me to pass on this message to you. He also said that it was of the greatest urgency."

Lord Blackmore scowled.

"I see." With a nod, he dismissed the footman and then looked back to his friends before turning to Rachael.

"It seems as though whoever said such a thing to that footman claimed to be Lord Kelling. The footman would not know if he was speaking the truth or not."

"That is true," Rachael agreed, quietly. "The footman is only a servant, and there are a good many gentlemen and ladies here. They must take such things as they are." Her eyes went to each gentleman in turn and then to Lord Blackmore himself. "What will you do?"

Lord Blackmore sighed and shook his head, pinching the bridge of his nose for a moment before dropping his hand.

"I do not know. If I do not do as is required, as is asked, then will not those who have been planning this know that I am aware of their schemes? And if I wish to discover them, then would it not be best that they continue to believe that I do not know anything of what they intend to do?"

"But you cannot go to that room alone!" Rachael exclaimed, fear beginning to rise up within her chest all over again. "If you do, then the gossip will begin to spread almost at once, I am sure of it!"

With a gentle smile, Lord Blackmore took her hand again, pressing it lightly for a moment.

"I have no intention of going anywhere alone, Miss Simmons, do not fear. Lord Richmond, Lord Elmsford, might you accompany me? After all," he finished, with a wry smile, "it is not as though that message stated that I was required to make my way there entirely alone!"

With relief, Rachael closed her eyes, swallowed, and nodded, glad now that there was to be no danger of him being caught up in this wicked scheme.

"But there is more here than I first thought," Lord Blackmore continued, his smile breaking apart. "Might I call on you soon, Miss Simmons? I think that there are some things we need to discuss."

Rachael blinked in surprise.

"I do not know if there is anything more that I can offer you, save for what I have told you already."

Lord Blackmore's smile returned quickly.

"All the same, I should like to be able to talk with you, Miss Simmons. Would you be willing to permit me to call on you?"

Her heart leapt but she quieted it at once.

"Of course. Thank you, Lord Blackmore."

"No, it is I who should be thanking you." With a smile, he inclined his head and then moved to the door. "I should go now. I am sure that these two men – whoever they are – will be watching for me."

"I will follow quietly thereafter," Rachael promised, as Lord Blackmore's eyes caught hers again. "It may be that I can see something more. Mayhap I will be able to see these men watching for you."

Lord Blackmore smiled.

"And here I thought that *I* would be the one to aid you, not the other way around," he said, making her smile. "Thank you, Miss Simmons. I am sure we will speak again very soon."

Rachael watched the three gentlemen step back out into the ballroom and after a few moments, followed them. Her heart was beating a little more quickly, her anxious thoughts rising up again but, as Lord Blackmore disappeared into the crowd, Rachael let her shoulders drop and quietened her pounding heart. There was no one following him, no one chasing him to make certain that he did as he had been asked. Thus far, those two gentlemen remained a mystery and Rachael could only pray that, soon, Lord Blackmore would be able to find out who they were – else the rest of this London Season could prove a very dangerous one for his reputation *and* his standing... and possibly her own.

CHAPTER SEVEN

Hugh walked with purpose and, though he kept his expression blank, his hands were pulled into tight fists, anger beginning to build with every step that he took. He was not angry in the least with Miss Simmons, of course, for he could give her nothing but relief and gratitude for the kindness and consideration she had shown him. Instead, his fury was directed at this invisible enemy, one who hid themselves away and, from the shadows, attempted to injure him by ruining his reputation – and for what cause? He had always been a respectable, honest gentleman and had never made any particular enemies – not that he knew of, at least. So why was someone attempting to tear him down with such strength?

And could it have continued from last Season? Was that first rumor meant to send me back to my estate to stay there?

"Lord Blackmore, good evening."

Hugh paused, clearing his throat gently as he bowed.

"Good evening, Miss Wilson. Might you excuse me for a few moments? I have been asked to go to speak with a particular gentleman, but I will return to your side in a few minutes."

Miss Wilson's eyes widened.

"Goodness, that sounds very serious indeed. Of course you must go." Her fan fluttered gently as her eyes dropped to the floor, only to lift to look up at him again. "I look forward to your return."

A warning edged into Hugh's heart and, though he returned her smile and moved away quickly, he silently reminded himself to be careful and cautious when it came to Miss Wilson. She appeared rather interested in his company and, though he found her quite agreeable, there was no return of interest there, not on his part.

"The parlor is off the corridor which is just through these doors." Lord Richmond, knowing their host's townhouse, indicated the double doors they were to walk through. "Though we will come with you, I will also watch for anyone who might be watching you."

"Thank you."

With a nod to Lord Elmsford, Hugh stepped through the doors and then made his way to the only door which was a little ajar, assuming it to be the parlor.

Stepping inside, with Lord Richmond and Lord Elmsford just behind him, Hugh was met by the open arms of a lady he did not recognize, her smile spreading wide across her face... only for her to then frown and step back, her arms dropping to her sides.

"You do not appear to be Lord Kelling," he said,

attempting to sound matter-of-fact. "I must be in the wrong room."

The lady's frown grew.

"You were looking for Lord Kelling?" Her frown began to fade away as her eyes opened a little wider. "Mayhap *he* is the gentleman I thought to be arriving here."

Lord Elmsford cleared his throat and caught her attention.

"You do not know who you are meeting, Lady Duthell?"

"I do not," she replied, no ounce of embarrassment in her expression. She was, Hugh recalled, meant to be as blithe as could be as regarded her standing here, and her personal preferences. Which meant she did not care what they thought of her. "I was only told by a footman that there was a gentleman requesting my company in the parlor."

Hugh spread out his hands, doing his best to put on an expression of regret.

"Alas, none of us are the gentleman who has requested your company, Lady Duthell. Forgive us for the intrusion. We must have all arrived at the wrong moment."

"But of course, I quite understand. I shall linger here, however, in the hope that he might appear!"

She laughed and, though Hugh did his best to smile, the realization of what might have occurred had he arrived in this parlor without his friends with him slammed hard into his mind. Shuddering lightly, he turned and made to step out of the room – only for the door to fling open and another gentleman to step inside.

"You there!" the newcomer exclaimed, his eyes wide and one finger pointing directly into Hugh's chest. "You have been..."

Hugh smiled to himself as the gentleman's eyes roved around the room, taking in not only Lady Duthell but also the presence of Lord Elmsford and Lord Richmond.

"Lord Locksley? Are you looking for Lady Duthell? She has been waiting for someone and I am afraid that it is not any of us!"

This suggestion made Lord Locksley's eyes flare wide and the hand which had been pointing directly at Hugh quickly fell back to his side.

"I – I am not."

"Then why are you in the parlor?" Lord Elmsford asked, sounding as innocent as might be, though Hugh knew all too well that the question was a pressing one, meant to try to uncover who had sent him here. Hugh watched the changing emotions flitting across the gentleman's face, silently wondering if *he* was the one who had been attempting to throw all manner of gossip around London, though quite why he would do so, Hugh did not know. They were barely acquainted.

"I was... that is to say, I heard that there was something of concern and I came to make certain that all was quite well." Lord Locksley drew himself up to his full height, though there was still a flicker in his eyes which did not fade. "It is a gentleman's duty to make certain that the lady is protected."

"Then you were concerned for Lady Duthell?" Lord

Elmsford asked, the question sending Lord Locksley's eyes wider than ever before. "That is very good of you, I must say. I did not think that the lady needed protecting."

"I certainly do not!" Lady Duthell stepped forward, her eyes flashing, though they softened when she took in Lord Locksley. "Though I am grateful for your concern, of course."

Hugh lifted an eyebrow, his eyes going from the lady to Lord Locksley and noting now the gentleman's face filled with color. Uncertain as to whether this gentleman was acquainted with Lady Duthell, he let himself smile as Lord Locksley simply nodded, made to say something and then, clearly thinking better of it, turned away.

"Well, that was very rude, I must say!" Lady Duthell pouted, her hands going to her hips. "What sort of gentleman ignores a lady such as myself?"

"I think he was a little embarrassed," Hugh replied, smiling at Lady Duthell. "But now that he has taken his leave, we must take ours also. Do excuse us."

Lady Duthell nodded, looking up at him again.

"Are you quite certain that you are not the gentleman I was meant to be meeting?"

"Alas, no." Hugh put one hand to his heart and kept his smile in place. "Would you wish for us to accompany you back to the ballroom?"

The lady let out a soft sigh and shook her head.

"No, thank you. For the moment, I think I shall linger here a little longer, just in case the gentleman – whoever he is – decides that he shall appear once you have all taken your leave."

Hugh smiled, excused himself again, and then left

the room, his friends following after him. It was not until they had returned to the ballroom, and each had picked up a drink from the tray held by one of the footmen that Hugh let his smile fade.

"That was all very carefully planned," he murmured, as Lord Elmsford nodded, and Lord Richmond took a sip of his brandy. "I do not know who sent Lord Locksley into that room and—"

"We could ask him."

Lord Elmsford immediately shook his head at Lord Richmond's suggestion.

"I do not think that the fellow would tell us. We have embarrassed him enough by making a connection between himself and Lady Duthell, and I do not think that he would tolerate any further questions, though we could try."

Hugh nodded.

"Try, Lord Richmond, if you wish. See what you can discover. Otherwise, I fear that we will continue to be as much in the dark as we are at present!"

His stomach began to twist this way and that and Hugh let out a slow breath, closing his eyes and trying to quieten the hurried beat of his heart. That had been a most disconcerting circumstance and one he might have walked into without any awareness, had it not been for Miss Simmons. Gratitude began to fill his heart, and he let out another slow breath, a coldness gripping him as he thought about what could have happened, had he believed that Lord Kelling truly was looking for him.

"You have a lot to thank Miss Simmons for."

Hugh glanced to Lord Elmsford, then nodded.

"I certainly do. I intend to call on her to see if there is anything more that she can tell me, anything more of interest. I shall, also, make my gratitude to her very clear indeed."

Lord Elmsford's lips twitched.

"There is a growing connection between the two of you, I think."

"Between myself and Miss Simmons?" Hugh shrugged, ignoring the note of curiosity in Lord Elmsford's voice. "I suppose it is to be expected, given that we have been caught up in the same rumor. It is clear now, however, that I am the one who is being set upon by this invisible assailant." A heaviness settled over his heart, and he let out a long sigh. "I do not know why someone is pursuing me with such dark intent. All I say is that, from this moment on, I intend to be a good deal more on my guard, in any and all situations."

"A wise thought."

"I do not truly understand what is happening," Lord Richmond put in, following Lord Elmsford's comment. "If you wished to explain it to me, then I should be grateful. At the present moment, it seems to me as though someone wishes to blacken your name, Blackmore, though I do not know why."

Hugh managed a small, wry smile.

"Neither do I," he stated, plainly. "But I fully intend to find out."

"Good afternoon, Miss Simmons." Hugh smiled warmly as he bowed towards the young lady. "I do hope that you are well?"

"I am, thank you." She gestured for him to sit down and took her seat again herself, leaving Hugh to follow suit. "My mother will return to join us very soon. An unexpected issue has arisen with a dinner party she is to hold tomorrow afternoon." She smiled, and Hugh watched the light flickers dance about in her eyes, immediately forgetting precisely why it was that he had come to call on her. Having stepped into the room, he had been immediately taken with the gentle smile on her lips and the clear happiness in her expression, wondering if her delight came from his own presence in the room. That sent a quiet joy into his heart, and he had instantly found his own spirits lifted – and that sensation had not left him as yet. "I do hope that the maid will suffice, for propriety's sake, in the meantime?"

Seeing the slight fading of her smile, Hugh quickly nodded.

"Of course! I am glad to hear that your mother is to hold a dinner party."

"As am I." Miss Simmons lifted both shoulders and then let them fall gently. "I am even more grateful to those who responded and accepted the invitation. I believe that my mother was rather concerned that many would not attend." Her smile faded a little more and she looked away. "There were those who refused."

"That is their own foolishness," Hugh responded, quickly. "Do not let your thoughts linger on that."

Miss Simmons' smile returned quickly, and warmth pooled in Hugh's stomach.

"Your wise words are appreciated, Lord Blackmore. You are quite right. I ought to be considering those who have accepted the invitation, rather than those who have not."

"Precisely. I have seen that you and the other wallflowers no longer linger in the shadows of the ballroom," Hugh continued, seeing a faint flush begin to dot her cheeks. "You are now walking through the ballroom arm in arm, forcing the other guests to take note of you. That is a considered action, I think?"

"It is." Her smile continued to send patches of light into her eyes. "Miss Bosworth has encouraged us not to act as wallflowers, not to permit those who look upon us as such to have their strength of opinion forced upon us. Therefore, we have been attempting to move through society as we did before, though many do not speak with us. Though," she continued, her lips twitching, "there are many whom I would not wish to speak with regardless, so that does not matter I suppose!"

Hugh laughed and saw her blushing, though her eyes danced.

"That is very good to hear, Miss Simmons. I congratulate you on your strength and determination! Miss Bosworth is quite correct, I think. You ought to be encouraged to step out into society as you have done before. If they do not acknowledge you, then the fault is theirs, not yours."

"I thank you." With a small smile, she looked away

just as the tea tray was brought in. "There are some advantages to being a wallflower, however."

"Such as being able to hide away and overhear something which might have otherwise ruined my reputation?"

Miss Simmons' gaze went to his.

"Yes, absolutely. You cannot know of my dread *and* my relief at hearing what I did. I was horrified that they would do such a thing but glad that I could then go to tell you about it. Might I ask what happened?"

Hugh watched her as she poured the tea, seeing the concern in how she glanced at him occasionally as she did so.

"If it had not been for you, Miss Simmons, I do not think that I would have been able to pull my reputation free from the mire into which it was intended to fall, should these men have had their way. It was just as you said. Lord Kelling required my urgent presence, I was told, and thus, I made my way to the parlor where he was supposedly waiting. Lord Elmsford and Lord Richmond were present with me and the three of us went into the room together. We did not find Lord Kelling but Lady Duthell, as you had overheard."

"And was she expecting you?"

With a dry chuckle, Hugh shook his head.

"No, she certainly was not! Her astonishment at our presence knew no bounds, Miss Simmons! She was expecting only one gentleman, not three!"

"Oh." Miss Simmons' face flushed again though her gaze, after she set the cup of tea down on the table near to him, was steady enough. "That is a relief, I suppose."

He frowned.

"In what way?"

"That she was not expecting you in particular," Miss Simmons explained, as Hugh's confusion began to fade. "Had she spoken aloud your name, then even with Lord Elmsford and Lord Richmond's presence, you might still have been presented with some difficulties as regarded your reputation."

Having not thought of this before this moment, Hugh swallowed hard and nodded, looking away.

"That is true indeed. I had not even considered that."

"But it is just as well she did not know if was to be you specifically," Miss Simmons said, picking up her tea and taking a sip. "So... what happened thereafter?"

"Lord Locksley appeared." Seeing her surprise, Hugh gave her a wry smile. "He made some bluster about it all, but was clearly expecting to see Lady Duthell in the arms of some gentleman... no doubt, myself! That was not what he came upon, however, and—"

To his surprise, Miss Simmons laughed, interrupting him.

"Forgive me," she said, her eyes twinkling. "I can only imagine the way he must have deflated, having expected to see one thing and being met with three gentlemen instead of the one!"

Hugh grinned.

"He was rather disconcerted, I must admit. I even suggested that he had come to the room to see Lady Duthell, that he was concerned for *her* welfare, and he was even more upset by that suggestion."

Miss Simmons laughed and shook her head, easing

the worries that had flung themselves into Hugh's mind as he had related all that had taken place.

"Goodness, that must have upset him a great deal! Though I do not mind, given that he was expecting to find you present, alone with the lady, and then did not!" Her smile began to disappear, the steady gaze returning. "Do you know who sent him to the parlor?"

"I do not. Lord Richmond is going to attempt to ask him, but I am not sure that Lord Locksley will be willing to speak. He was already rather embarrassed."

"Let us hope that he will."

Hugh nodded, then leaned forward in his chair, wanting to make certain that he spoke honestly and openly before her mother returned.

"Miss Simmons, I came not only to tell you what happened, and to ask you if you recalled anything more, but also to ask if you might be willing to offer your help."

Her eyes rounded.

"Help you? What is it that you wish me to do?"

Spreading his hands, Hugh gave a small, rueful smile.

"I am quite at a loss as to who is doing this, Miss Simmons. I do not know which person is attempting to seek me out, why they are trying to ruin my reputation utterly, and unfortunately, bring you into the situation also. I must discover them. I must find out who it is who is doing this and the reasons behind it. Otherwise, I shall never be contented, I shall always be looking over my shoulder and wondering who it is pursuing me. I may very well fall into whatever trap it is they have set for me, for I do not believe that what happened last evening was their first and only attempt."

Miss Simmons frowned, biting her lip for a moment before she answered, clearly carefully considering what it was that he was asking of her.

"You believe that someone is seeking to ruin you purposefully," she said, as Hugh nodded. "But you have no particular enemies? You have never done anything which might make a situation between yourself and another a difficult one?" Hugh shook his head no. "From what I understand, you have always had a sterling reputation, save for what was suggested of you last Season," she continued, a gentle line marring her forehead. "And now someone is doing their utmost to take that from you, though you do not know why."

"That is it, precisely. I am only sorry that you have been involved also," Hugh added, as she offered him a small smile. "I do not know why your name was brought to the fore, but mayhap it was simply the case that the *ton* made a connection which was not truly there and thus, you suffered."

Miss Simmons' eyes darkened for a few moments.

"It would not be the first time that the *ton* had made a mistake when it comes to gossip."

"Then will you help me, Miss Simmons? I am not certain of what it is that I intend to do, as yet, but I should like to have you beside me when it comes to seeking out answers. You say that being a wallflower does have its advantages – well, mayhap those advantages might be put to good use as we try to discover the truth."

He held his breath as Miss Simmons nodded slowly, her fingers at her lips, her eyes roving around the room as she thought about what it was that he was asking of her.

If she did not accept then, yes, Hugh admitted, he would be disappointed, though he would never demand anything from her.

Then, Miss Simmons smiled, and Hugh let out a long breath, hope beginning to burn in his chest.

"Yes, I will help you." Miss Simmons shrugged lightly. "After all, this has affected my own reputation also, and anything I can do to assist, not only you but also myself, can only be a good thing. Whatever it is that you wish me to do, I am more than willing."

Hugh smiled broadly, his heart quickening with both gratitude and relief.

"Thank you, Miss Simmons. This means more to me than I believe I can express."

Glancing to the door and hearing footsteps, he quickly rose to greet Lady Grant, relieved that he had been able to speak to Miss Simmons alone but, try as he might, he could not keep his gaze on the older lady. Instead, his eyes continually returned to Miss Simmons, his heart leaping in his chest every time he set his gaze on her. Courageous, strong, and determined, she had offered him the support he required and together, he was sure, they would be able to find out the truth.

CHAPTER EIGHT

Rachael smiled as she greeted her friends.
"Good evening to you. How does this evening fare thus far?"

"It is better now that you have arrived." Miss Fairley smiled and gestured to the rest of the room. "We were just about to take a turn about the room. Do you wish to join us?"

"But of course." Rachael looked around, her smile disappearing. "But where is Miss Bosworth?"

Miss Fairley smiled, her eyes warm.

"She is gone with another gentleman! She is taking company with Lord Yarmouth which I am glad for, though there are some questions over... well, I suppose such a thing does not matter at the present moment, not when you have your own concerns!"

Rachael offered her a wry smile.

"I am doing my very best not to become overwhelmed by what Lord Blackmore has asked of me."

As she had spoken to her friends about the matter

already, Miss Fairley knew what she spoke of and offered her a warm, encouraging smile.

"You will be able to be of significant help to him, I am sure," she said, smiling. "Has he asked you anything specific as yet?"

"No, only that if I see anything or hear anything more, to go to him at once. I believe that he is very concerned."

"As one would be, knowing that there is someone determined to pull your name into disrepute!" Lady Frederica exclaimed. "It does seem very strange. After all, Lord Blackmore has – or had – a stellar reputation, though it is a little tainted after the rumors which came from last Season, as regards your presence at his house – and he is also a gentleman with no particular enemies! I cannot understand why anyone would desire to injure him so. It does not make any particular sense, not to my mind at least."

"They must want something from him," Rachael mused, aloud. "They must see that there is benefit in him losing his standing and his reputation and that, in some way, is of benefit to this person, whoever they may be."

Her friends nodded but nothing else came to the fore. Rachael grimaced, wishing that she could find something practical to do that might be to Lord Blackmore's advantage, but she could not. Yes, she could continue to watch and to listen, which was something she was able to do all the more, given her standing as a wallflower, but was there not something else she could do? Something which might aid him more?

"He is a very handsome gentleman."

A little startled, Rachael looked back at her friend, seeing Miss Fairley's eyes glinting.

"I beg your pardon?"

"Lord Blackmore," Miss Fairley said, pointedly. "He is a handsome gentleman, is he not? And very kind."

Rachael nodded slowly, aware of the slow curling warmth in her chest as she considered Lord Blackmore.

"I would agree, of course."

"And there is already a connection spoken of between you," Lady Frederica added, making Rachael frown. "Might you think that there could be... something of a profound connection there between you?"

Immediately shaking her head no, Rachael tried to push away the idea which had come rushing into her mind the very second her friend had spoken.

"No, I cannot think so."

"And why not?"

Lady Frederica's blunt question had Rachael stumbling, trying to find an answer.

"Because... because he has come to me for help, not for anything else! Yes, I might think him handsome, and he is certainly kind, I will not pretend he is not, but I cannot let myself think or even imagine any other such thing!"

Lady Frederica and Miss Fairley shared a glance – a glance which had them both smiling broadly.

"And why ever not?" Miss Fairley asked, though with a good deal more gentleness than Lady Frederica. "There is nothing wrong with considering a connection to Lord Blackmore. If he is a good gentleman, which you believe him to be, then what could be your reason for pushing that away?"

Rachael threw up her hands, all too aware of the twisting tightness in her chest which was threatening to overwhelm her.

"Because I cannot! I am much too focused on what there is threatening him – threatening me also – to permit my mind to think on any other thing."

"That does not mean that there is not a flicker of interest in your mind, however," Lady Frederica laughed, though Rachael blushed furiously. "If you find him an interesting gentleman, if you are drawn to him, then there is no need to make a secret of it. We shall not think worse of you for it."

Rachael shook her head.

"Truly, I am only thinking of these rumors and how best to free ourselves from them," she promised, though neither of her friends appeared to believe her, given the looks on their faces. "It is a concern! After all, that is why I am a wallflower."

This brought the smiles on her friends' faces crashing down and, though Rachael did not like to see it, she looked back at them steadily, the truth burning through the air between them and severing all joviality.

"I do not say such a thing because I am overly sorrowful," she continued, quietly, "as I am grateful for what I have been given. I have friends and I have found a new, slow-growing courage thanks to Miss Bosworth – and to all of you. But I would much prefer *not* to be looked upon in such a way, especially given that I have done nothing to deserve it."

"I can understand that." Miss Fairley smiled gently, no doubt to reassure Rachael that she did not feel any upset whatsoever. "There must be a strong desire to remove these rumors from you so that you can regain your standing."

"And find a good match," Lady Frederica added, though the glint in her eye remained. "There is a gentleman within your sphere who might very well already *be* a good match for you, my dear friend. All you have to do is consider it."

With a wry smile, Rachael said nothing but turned her head to look out at the small, gathered crowd. They were not at a ball this evening, but rather a soiree, though they were just as ignored as usual. Much to her surprise, her thoughts lingered on Lord Blackmore. Even though she had told her friends that she had no time nor inclination to think about anything aside from how to remove these rumors from both herself and from Lord Blackmore, she found her thoughts lingering on him, thinking about the way he had smiled at her, the softness about his green eyes as he had watched her.

A delightful shiver ran through her frame, and she closed her eyes as if to hold the vision to herself, to cling to it a little longer.

"Is he here this evening?"

Rachael opened her eyes and was about to tell her friend that she did not know whether or not Lord Blackmore was present as yet, only to realize that it was not one of them who was speaking.

"I do not know." Another lady's voice, a little higher pitched than the first, was clear to Rachael's hearing and she slowly looked all about her, only to realize that the two ladies speaking were standing only a short distance from them all, though they were separated by a bookcase which sat flat against the wall beside them. Sighing to herself at how quickly and how easily a wallflower could be forgotten, Rachael went to turn to her friends to suggest that they take their leave, only for Lord Blackmore's name to catch her attention.

"It was said that Blackmore was found with Lady Duthell, though there were other gentlemen there also."

A snort came from the second lady.

"A most unfortunate incident. They ought to have been a good deal more careful."

Frowning, Rachael glanced at Lady Frederica and then to Miss Fairley, but both looked as confused as she felt. Either these ladies, whoever they were, might be speaking in connection with the gentlemen who had attempted to trap Lord Blackmore into a situation with Lady Duthell, *or* they were speaking in support of Lord Blackmore.

As yet, she did not know.

"There is also the suggestion that he is poverty-stricken, though I do not think that can be true," the first said, sniffing. "It seems that this ball is to be the most wonderful, ostentatious affair of the Season thus far! And someone who was poverty-stricken would be sunk in despair, not holding extravagant balls!"

The second lady murmured something which Rachael could not make out and, though she strained to hear, there was nothing in particular which could be overheard. The first lady laughed – though it was not a kind sound – and then moved away from the bookcase, ready to walk past Rachael and her friends without seeing her.

Before she knew what she was doing, Rachael stepped forward, out of the shadows, and almost collided with the lady in question. The first lady's eyes flared wide.

"Do forgive me! I did not mean to step into your path."

The first lady recoiled, while the second let out an exclamation of frustration and stepped back, though her brown eyes narrowed, and her jaw tightened as she glared at Rachael.

"You should watch where you are going! How dare you think to–"

"If you are looking for Lord Blackmore, I have not yet seen him present here this evening," Rachael interrupted, her stomach twisting this way and that as she spoke with both boldness and courage, making it quite plain to the ladies that she had overheard them speaking. "Because of our standing as wallflowers, we do tend to see who comes into a house and who takes their leave, and we have not seen him as yet."

She smiled in what she hoped appeared to be a rather innocent manner, but the two ladies only blinked, with the second one slowly beginning to turn a little pale. Her blonde curls bounced gently as she looked to the first, clearly considering what it was that they would say in response.

Perhaps their remarks had not been meant to be overheard.

"I – I do not think–"

"I thank you." With a smile that did not send any light up into her eyes, the first lady moved a little in front of the second, who was now beginning to bluster and nodded to Rachael. "You are very kind."

"We did not mean to overhear, of course," Lady Frederica added with what was clearly meant to be a charming smile. "It is one of the downfalls of being forced to stay at the back of every room. We hear a good many things without ever having intended to do so!"

"We quite understand," the first lady said, with what sounded like a trace of warmth in her voice, though the second lady appeared to be furious, given the redness in her cheeks. "It does not matter. We were only speaking of Lord Blackmore due to the gossip which has been spreading through society about him of late."

Lady Frederica glanced at Rachael though she kept her smile pinned in place.

"Most understandable. Should you like us to inform him that you were both looking for him, should he arrive? I do not think that he would mind a wallflower telling him such a thing as that."

The lady's eyes flared, and she shook her head, pressing her lips tight together.

"No, thank you. That is not necessary."

"Not necessary in the least!" the second exclaimed, as Rachael kept her smile fixed, wondering at their sudden, forceful reaction. "Good evening to you!"

The first lady did not rush off as quickly as the second had done, however. Instead, she murmured her good evening and inclined her head before stepping away, though Rachael narrowed her gaze just a little as she watched them both walk away.

"That was a little unusual." Looking at Miss Fairley, she watched her friend nod slowly, with Lady Frederica doing the same. "I wonder what they meant."

"It is a little unusual for them to be speaking of Lord Blackmore and Lady Duthell," Lady Frederica murmured, her forehead still puckered. "Not a great many gentlemen or ladies knew of that – or at least, I thought they did not."

Rachael caught her lip between her teeth for a few moments, considering.

"It may be that Lord Elmsford, Lord Kelling, or Lord Richmond have said something to others and thus, the news has spread around society... though I would find that a little surprising, given that they are his friends and would know that he is doing his utmost to keep gossip away from him."

Miss Fairley nodded.

"Precisely." She looked at Rachael, one eyebrow lifting. "Will you inform him?"

"Inform who?"

"Lord Blackmore. I think that you should tell him what it is that you have overheard. He might know one or both of these ladies and, even if nothing comes of the conversation, he should know of it at least."

Rachael considered and then agreed.

"I shall have to find him first! It is as I said to those two ladies, I have not seen him yet."

"You have been looking for him though, yes?" Again, came the twinkling smile to Lady Frederica's face and

Rachael blushed, though again, chose to say nothing and permit her silence to be the answer she gave. Lady Frederica laughed softly and then looped her arm through Rachael's. "There is nothing you need be embarrassed about and, indeed, I will stop teasing you now. Forgive me." With a smile, she nudged Rachael lightly. "Should you like to take a walk around the house? Mayhap we shall see him that way."

"Very well." It did not take a lot of persuasion for Rachael to agree, and whether Lady Frederica recognized that or not, she said not a word. Together, with Miss Fairley with them, the three ladies set out for a short walk around the house, with Rachael still thinking of all that she had heard from those two, as yet unknown, ladies... and wondering just what Lord Blackmore would make of it all.

CHAPTER NINE

Lord Kelling stuck one elbow into Hugh's ribs and he immediately grimaced. "Good heavens, whatever was that for?"

"To stop you from keeping that expression pinned to your face given that we are about to walk past some ladies," came the reply. "You *are* aware that you have been scowling, are you not?"

Hugh cleared his throat and looked away, the sunshine warming his face. Managing to smile at the ladies they passed, ladies who were also enjoying the fine summer's day in St James' Park, he threw a look to Lord Kelling.

"I was unaware of my expression."

"You have something on your mind."

"Of course I do!" Hugh exclaimed, turning back to look at his friend. "My ball is tomorrow evening, and I have been so caught up with all that must be done with it, I have been unable to attend one or two social occasions and, all the while, I have been thinking about what might be said about me or what it is that society thinks of me at present!"

Lord Kelling looked suddenly serious.

"I quite understand. Forgive me, I did not mean to be flippant."

With a sigh, Hugh closed his eyes briefly, a little irritated at his own sharp response.

"Forgive me for being so sharp," he responded with a wry smile. "There has been a good deal on my mind of late."

What he did not mention to his friend was that, in the midst of all of this, he had been unable to stop thinking of Miss Simmons for, given their last conversation had been about what they might be able to accomplish together, it had been a little frustrating that he had been unable to speak with her since! They had agreed that their minds would be aligned in an attempt to find out who it was that was trying to spread rumors and gossip throughout London – and pulling her name into it in the meantime – but there had been nothing decided, nothing said other than the promise that should she hear or see anything more, she would tell him at once. Hugh wanted to do more, wanted to find a way for them to truly pursue his tormentor but, as yet, he could not think of what to do. It would be a lie to say that she had not been in his thoughts, for she had been almost ever-present, even when he had been in the midst of his preparations.

"There has been a good deal of talk about your upcoming ball," Lord Kelling told him, making Hugh scowl. "It seems to have done as you had hoped and put the rumors about gambling away your fortune to bed.

There will be many coming who hope that all they have heard whispered about your ball will be exactly as they have heard!"

Hugh chuckled, though he shook his head with it.

"Given the sheer amount of coin I have had to spend on this ball, I should say that it shall be! I–"

Frowning, he came to a stop, something catching his attention. From where he stood, it seemed to be that three or four ladies were surrounding one young lady who, given the way that she recoiled, did not much appreciate their nearness.

His gut twisted.

"Mayhap we ought to go *this* way," he said, seeing Lord Kelling frown. "We will be able to speak to the young ladies present, at the very least."

"Indeed. Though I do wonder where the young lady's chaperone is." Musing aloud, Lord Kelling fell into step beside him. "Mayhap she is nearby and cannot see – or does not realize – that this is not a good situation."

Hugh's eyebrows drew together as they grew closer, quickly realizing that the young lady who was continually pulling back from the others – though she was now near to a small copse of trees and unable to move away any further – was none other than Miss Simmons.

His heart kicked hard, and he quickened his pace.

"It is quite clear that Lord Blackmore does not want anything to do with you!" he heard some young lady exclaim. "Your name continually attaches to his and it is unwanted! It is undesirable! Why you should *think* to attach yourself to such a gentleman after the shame you have brought upon yourself, I cannot know!"

"It will not lift you from the shadows, if that is what you think," said another – one Hugh recognized to be none other than Miss Wilson. "It seems to me that someone is whispering about Lord Blackmore in the hope that his reputation will worsen so terribly that he will be forced to marry someone of lesser standing, someone less worthy of a connection to him, and, the more I think of this, the more I wonder if it is *you* who are doing so," Miss Wilson finished, her head tossing back in a flourish of triumph. "Is that what all of this is about, Miss Simmons? You seek to marry Lord Blackmore but, given that he has been cleared of whatever shame you sought to place on him *last* Season, you cannot reach him again. Therefore, you are doing all you can to blacken his reputation again so that you might place yourself beside him!"

Much to Hugh's horror, the nods of agreement and the murmurs concurring with Miss Wilson came much too quickly for his liking and, as he drew near, he saw how pale the face of Miss Simmons was.

"Good afternoon." Speaking with great strength, Hugh looked around the group, taking in not only Miss Wilson, with whom he was acquainted, but also Lady Joceline and Lady Tabitha. They all returned his gaze with a slight rounding of their eyes, clearly having not expected him to appear. "I was certain that I heard my name being spoken." Looking over his shoulder to Lord Kelling, he lifted an eyebrow. "Did you hear my name, Lord Kelling?"

"I did." The gentleman came to stand beside Hugh, his arms clasping in front of him though he did not smile.

"It is a great pity to see that so many beautiful and refined young ladies of the *ton* are so willing to engage in gossip."

"Oh, but we are not engaging in gossip, Lord Kelling," Miss Wilson exclaimed, quickly. "We are only speaking to Miss Simmons, explaining to her that she ought to be keeping to her place." The sharpness of her eyes made Hugh wince, hardly able to imagine what it must feel like for Miss Simmons at present to be spoken so. "It is not right for her—"

"Miss Simmons is doing nothing wrong," he interrupted, looking at her for the first time and a little surprised to see the ice in her gaze – though, he presumed, it was not directed at him. "I cannot imagine what it is that you are placing upon her shoulders at present, Miss Wilson, for there is nothing she has done against me."

Miss Wilson opened her mouth to respond, but before she could do so, Lady Tabitha spoke up.

"She is attempting to ruin you, Lord Blackmore, surely you can see that?"

"In what way?"

Lady Tabitha's lip curled.

"In spreading these rumors about you, she is placing herself to be your only viable consideration when it comes to matrimony."

"I have done no such thing." For the first time, Miss Simmons spoke up and when Hugh looked at her, her face was white, her eyes sharp but her voice steady and firm. "You have made that up solely from your own thoughts," she continued, her voice cutting through the air clearly, though many of the young ladies sneered and tossed their heads as if dismissing her words without thought. "From the beginning, my name has been pulled into this and–"

"If you are speaking about your *disgrace* from last Season, then I must interrupt you," Lady Joceline stated, her face pulled into a mask of dislike. "*You* chose to behave in such a way as that, Miss Simmons, and for whatever reason, the *ton* mistakenly believed that it was Lord Blackmore's townhouse from which you escaped. We know now it was not his townhouse but some other gentleman's and yet, you continue to deny that it was you! Surely it would be best to be honest about the situation *and* your attempts now to coerce Lord Blackmore into marrying you by making his disgrace seem to be the same as yours!"

"That is all nonsense." Miss Simmons took a step forward and, though her hands were tight, her voice was measured if not a little louder than before. "I did not step into any gentleman's townhouse alone, nor did I leave it in the early morning! I have no intention of trying to coerce Lord Blackmore into anything and I certainly have not said a single word against him."

"No, she has not." Hugh spoke up again, his anger beginning to burn at the way these ladies were speaking to Miss Simmons and at the disgrace they were throwing at her when there was nothing that she had done which was wrong. He had to say something, had to make it quite plain that he did not agree with anything they said about the lady. "Miss Simmons and I are well acquainted, and I can assure you that she has not taken part in any rumors or any gossipmongering as yet."

Lady Josephine smirked.

"You are a little foolish, Lord Blackmore, if you believe that a lady could not be sweetness when they are in your company and thereafter, speak ill of you in private."

"I know Miss Simmonds," Hugh retorted, firmly. "And I have not even a single thought in my mind that she would do such a thing as that. You may think that you have the entire matter making sense in your own minds, but I can assure you, you are nothing short of mistaken."

Another murmur ran around the group and Hugh glanced at Miss Simmons, catching the faint hint of red which now ran into her cheeks. He offered her a small smile, but Miss Simmons did not return it. Perhaps her emotions were already much too overwhelmed.

"Are you trying to state that there is more between yourself and Miss Simmons?" Lady Tabitha moved closer to him, keeping her eyes trained on his face, though there was a slightly pinched look about her expression. "I will admit to seeing you in conversation with her on one or two occasions, and confess myself to be a little surprised about such a thing. After all, why would a gentleman such as yourself be eager to speak with someone whose name has been connected to their own in such a way?"

Hugh kept his gaze steady, feeling the weight of the group's eyes upon him and all too aware of Miss Simmons' presence beside him. His heart began to thunder as he took in a slow breath and gave what he hoped was a measured response.

"The reason I would be glad to speak to Miss Simmons is because she has done nothing wrong," he said, his words crisp through the clear afternoon air. "She did not step out of my townhouse, nor out of anyone else's townhouse. She has no desire to trap me in matrimony and has no interest in spreading any rumors. Indeed, the only thing she seeks – as I do also – is to remove this burden from our shoulders. We do not want the *ton* to view us with blurred vision, to see us through the lens of lies and whispers – lies and whispers which have been perpetrated by those who are willing still to spread them without consideration." With a slight tilt of his chin, Hugh narrowed his gaze just a fraction, seeing Lady Tabitha's face flush hot. His point was quite clear. "I will speak to whomever I please, Lady Tabitha, and that shall include Miss Simmons because she is just as much a lady of society as many others. Indeed, I find myself greatly enjoying her company and I look forward to continuing in that connection, regardless of what anyone else might think of it."

Lady Tabitha's eyes flashed angrily.

"What I think of it, Lord Blackmore, is that you are ensnared by Miss Simmons, a lady who seeks to lie and to whisper and to deceive, all so that she might attract the attention of the only gentleman she might be able to marry."

"Then you are wrong," Hugh responded, his anger burning now. "She would not need to do so – no need to do anything like that at all."

Her arms folded across her chest, Lady Tabitha laughed mockingly, shaking her head at him.

"And what reason would that be, Lord Blackmore?"

"Because we are already betrothed!"

The words flew out of his mouth before he had a chance to stop them. Breathing hard, he saw Lady Tabitha recoil, her hands falling to her sides, her eyes wide and staring, mouth slack and color pulling from her cheeks in only an instant.

"Upon my return to London, I saw how the *ton* treated Miss Simmons in comparison to how they treated me," Hugh continued, giving himself no time, no opportunity to think about what it was that he had said, but rather forcing himself on regardless, "and I felt it my duty to offer her my hand. After all, she has done no wrong, and yet the *ton* chose to dismiss her, to push her to the very back of society, whilst treating me as though there was nothing amiss!"

Swallowing, he dared a glance at Miss Simmons, but she had gone very still, her head dropping forward as she stared down at her hands. He could not get even a glimpse of her expression. "I have not spoken of it before now, because I wanted to do everything that we could to try to free Miss Simmons from the burden the *ton* has placed upon her. If she was able to be restored, then our betrothal would come to an end, and she would be free to marry whomever she wished. Now, however, I see that such a hope is never to be ignited and thus, I do not need to keep this back from anyone any longer."

Taking in a deep breath, he lifted his chin and looked around the assembled group, seeing now that it had grown a little larger. Evidently, his proclamation had garnered the interest of others. "Yes, I am betrothed to Miss Rachael Simmons, and we are to be married by the end of the year. So, Lady Tabitha, Lady Joceline, and

Miss Wilson, there could be no reason for Miss Simmons to do or say anything akin to what you have suggested. She is not responsible for any sin against me. She has not gossiped, whispered, or tried to pull my reputation away from me. That would be foolish, would it not, as she is to be my wife?" With a small smile, and ignoring the pain which came with the thundering of his heart, he offered his arm to Miss Simmons, praying that she would take it. "When you speak ill of my betrothed when you place guilt upon her shoulders which she does not deserve, you can be certain that you injure me also – and I will not stand to hear such words against her. I do hope that is now quite clear to you all."

Tentative fingers touched his arm and, turning, Hugh began to walk away from the small group, relieved when Miss Simmons' hand rested all the more firmly on his arm. A glance behind him told him that Lord Kelling had begun to follow, though it was not until they were some distance away from them that Lord Kelling began to speak.

"Good gracious, old boy! I did not know... my heartiest congratulations!"

Hugh could barely bring himself to glance at Miss Simmons, his own heart beating furiously, sweat breaking out across his forehead as he realized not only what he had done, but also what this now meant for both his and *her* future.

"My mother is just there." Miss Simmons' voice was tight, and she did not look at him. "Thank you, Lord Blackmore. I am able to make my way to her myself."

He put her hand over hers as it sat on his arm, effectively pinning her to him for a moment, forcing her eyes to meet his.

"Miss Simmons, there is much we must discuss."

The blue of her eyes shifted for a moment, sending dark, shadowy streaks right through them as she frowned, looking away from him.

"I am aware of that, Lord Blackmore, but I must beg for some time to consider what has taken place. It is overwhelming. You must understand that."

Swallowing, Hugh dropped his head.

"I do. I did not mean... that is to say, I had no expectation of saying such a thing, Miss Simmons."

"But now that it is said, it is impossible for us to step back from it," she replied, quietly. "Let us both take some time to consider what this means. Mayhap you might think about coming to call on me soon, so we might discuss it?"

"Of course. But will you be in attendance at my ball tomorrow evening?"

She looked up at him and pressed her lips flat.

"I suppose I cannot hide myself away now, given that I am your betrothed."

The word on her lips sent a flurry of sensation through Hugh, though he did not know exactly what the feeling was, nor where it came from.

"I am glad that you will still attend. Forgive me for the difficulties I have caused by speaking without truly thinking of what would follow. It was not my intention. My intention was to aid you."

A tiny flickering smile pulled at her lips – but only for a moment.

"I understand, Lord Blackmore." At this, her hand pulled from his arm, and she began to walk away, only to turn around to look at him again. "There was something I wished to tell you, unrelated to our betrothal. There was a conversation I overheard at a soiree some two days ago, one where you were not present, and the conversation was... a little concerning. I–"

"Lord Blackmore!"

Hugh caught the flare in Miss Simmons' eyes, just before he turned himself to see who it was calling his name. Not recognizing the fellow, Hugh frowned and looked back, but Miss Simmons had already hurried away from him and had returned to her mother.

"You were not betrothed before this moment?" Lord Kelling asked, his voice quiet and eyes filled with surprise. "Good gracious, Blackmore, whatever were you thinking?"

Hugh closed his eyes as the gentleman calling his name drew ever closer.

"In truth, Kelling, I was not thinking clearly at all. I wanted to protect Miss Simmons, to have the *ton* stop speaking these incredibly damning things and, somehow, I found myself stating that we were already betrothed as a reason for her not to have done what they accused her of."

Lord Kelling let out a low whistle of surprise.

"Goodness. I shall offer you my congratulations nonetheless, however, for I think Miss Simmons, from what I have heard, is a decent young lady. You cannot step back from this – or from her – now, you are aware of that, yes?"

With a nod, Hugh turned to face the approaching

gentleman, seeing three ladies hurrying behind him. Clearly, news about his betrothal had spread fast.

"I have no intention of stepping away from my betrothal," he declared, firmly. "I fully intend to marry Miss Simmons and make her my wife, just as I have stated."

With a polite smile on his face, Hugh began to answer the many questions the gentlemen and ladies started to throw at him. All the while, however, his heart began to lift, happiness settling through it and, as he considered what it would be like to stand up in church and take Miss Simmons as his wife, a joy began to fill him, making his spirits rise and his smile broad.

Perhaps this moment of thoughtlessness would bring him more happiness than he had ever imagined.

CHAPTER TEN

Rachael blinked hot tears out of her eyes, shock ricocheting through her as she reached her mother.

"Mama. We must return to the carriage. Now."

Her mother looked at her with a frown, though she hurried along the path beside Rachael without so much as a word of protest.

"Do not tarry, I beg of you."

"It is still some time until your friends are to join us for afternoon tea," Lady Grant reminded her, making Rachael shake her head, her breath coming in quick pants as she rounded the corner that would lead them back to the gate and the waiting carriage. "You do not need to worry. I am sorry that I stepped away from you for a few minutes, but Lady Armitage and I fell into such a deep conversation that I quite lost myself! Were you quite all right? I saw you walking with a gentleman and–"

"No, Mama, I was not quite all right."

Tears began to splash onto Rachael's cheeks and her

mother instantly caught her breath in a gasp of surprise and shock, taking Rachael's hand and catching her so she might pull her back and look into her face. Rachael could not stop her tears now, even though they were still in the middle of the park and, though her mother asked her what was wrong, she could not get the words out.

"Whatever has happened, we must get you back to the carriage," Lady Grant murmured, thrusting a handkerchief in Rachael's direction, and then putting her hand through Rachael's arm so that she might almost pull her along the path. "It is not far. Look, there are three ladies approaching. Pray, drop your head so that they will not see your tears."

Rachael did as she was asked and, much to her relief, the three ladies walked past her without a word, though they did murmur a greeting in Lady Grant's direction. Her vision blurred with fresh tears, shock still chasing through her as she fought to find even a small semblance of composure. It was too difficult to find, too distant a thing to cling to and so, she struggled on, her breath tight and her chest heaving.

I am betrothed.

She did not know whether she cried from shock or relief. Lord Blackmore was a good man, with a fine character and a kindness in him which she valued. If she were to be honest with herself, she would admit that her desire to be close to him had grown considerably, though she had done her best to ignore such an awareness and to set it to one side, given her present circumstances. Now, however, those circumstances had grown all the more difficult, and she was left in the middle of it all, doing her utmost to find a way to regain some of her poise, rather than being flustered and upset.

"What happened?" Lady Grant waited until Rachael had been helped up into the carriage before coming to join her, sitting down opposite, and looking Rachael straight in the eye. "I should not have left you. I should not have become so distracted that—"

"I do not blame you," Rachael managed, in between hiccoughs and sobs. "It was not your fault, Mama. I was surrounded by a small group of ladies, all of whom were quite determined to cast me into despair." Her eyes closed as fresh tears fell to her cheeks. "They stated that I *was* guilty of the shame placed upon me last Season. It might not have been Lord Blackmore's townhouse, but it *was* the townhouse of a gentleman, they said. Thereafter, they stated that *I* have been the one spreading gossip and the like about Lord Blackmore, in the hope that he will be brought low and thus, I will be the only one ready to step in beside him as his wife." Lady Grant turned her head away sharply, her eyes at the window, one hand at her mouth. Shaking her head, she made to say something, only to think better of it. "Lord Blackmore and his friend were walking together at the same time as this was said," Rachael continued, softly, her tears subsiding as the truth began to sink into her soul. "They overheard all of this and came to my defense. Lord Blackmore stated that he and I were acquainted, he knew full well that I would do no such thing… but then another lady told him that he was a fool and that I was speaking kindly to him in his company but ill of him thereafter."

"How could they?" Lady Grant's head whipped

around, her face white, her eyes blazing with anger. "How *dare* they say such things as that? That is all entirely untrue, all made up by their imaginations and yet spoken as though it is quite true!"

Rachael nodded and sighed.

"I know, Mama." What she was to say next began to wriggle up through her towards her heart, sending a nervousness sparking through her. "As I said, Lord Blackmore came to my defense, though I also spoke in my own." Gripping the handkerchief in both hands, she looked down at it, took in a deep breath, and then spoke the words that would change the course of her life forever. "He told the assembled group that I would have no reason to speak ill of him, that I had no cause to do such a thing as they threw at me, for the sole reason that we..." Closing her eyes tightly, she let out a shuddering breath. "We are already betrothed."

Her mother's gasp was the only response Rachael expected. There came, thereafter, nothing but silence, and when Rachael opened her eyes to look back at her mother, Lady Grant was staring at her, her eyes rounded and one hand at her mouth.

Rachael could only nod, to confirm to her mother that what she had overheard was quite true, and Lady Grant's eyes flooded with tears. What Rachael did not expect, however, was for her mother to start laughing, tears dropping to her cheeks as she reached across to grasp Rachael's hand.

"This is wonderful news! You are betrothed? To Lord Blackmore?"

Nodding, Rachael could not rid herself of the tightness in her throat, a little surprised at how overjoyed her mother appeared to be.

"Had he intentions of asking for your hand, do you think?" Lady Grant asked, still squeezing Rachael's hand while her other hand wiped at her cheeks. "Was this always his intention and, in that one moment, found himself unable to do anything other than state what he had always hoped would be?"

"I – I could not say, Mama." Still a little stunned by how happy her mother was, Rachael took in a deep breath and then let it out again slowly, "You think that it is a good thing then?"

"How could it not be?" Lady Grant threw up her hands, having released Rachael's. "What I have hoped for, what I feared would never happen, has now come about, and with such a good gentleman as Lord Blackmore! How wonderful! Do you know when the wedding shall be?"

With a pause, Rachael reached across, grasped her mother's hands, and looked straight back into her face.

"Mama, I need you to listen to me. I am shocked – nay, stunned, by this. I did not expect him to say such a thing and, indeed, I do not think that *he* thought he would say such a thing either! We have not had the opportunity to speak together as yet, to understand what must happen next, or even to see how we feel about our impending marriage. After all, it came as such a surprise, I do not think that even Lord Blackmore himself realizes what he has done!"

Lady Grant smiled, though her enthusiasm was a little dampened now, much to Rachael's relief.

"I understand fully, my dear. However, nothing can be done to change this, not unless you both wish to bring a great scandal to London, and I am certain that is the last thing that Lord Blackmore wishes for! Therefore, you must now begin to prepare for your upcoming marriage to him, whether that be in your own heart and mind first, and in practical preparations thereafter, it does not matter. You are *betrothed*, Rachael! You are to be married, you will be mistress of an estate and, with any hope, mother to the heir of Blackmore. Is that not something worth being happy about? Something which you might sing for sheer joy over?"

Rachael considered her mother's words, sensing the shock beginning to fade away the more she thought about what she would gain by becoming Lord Blackmore's wife. Her heart began to quicken as she wondered whether he might, one day, pull her into his arms as, she supposed, any husband would.

He does not know that I am drawn to him.

Her quiet smile began to fade as she blinked, tears still in the edges of her eyes. While she knew she ought to be glad about her betrothal, while she ought to find happiness in the knowledge that she would have a secure future, the realization that what she felt for Lord Blackmore might remain hidden for some time – if not forever – bit down on her heart and sent a shock of pain rippling through her.

Her feelings for him would not disappear, of that she was quite certain. After all, she was to be spending more time in his company, was she not? As his wife, she would have a closer, more intimate acquaintance than ever before. Could she truly believe that her feelings would fade? No, certainly they would grow into something more profound than she had ever imagined possible.

"Your friends will be both surprised and, I am sure, delighted for you also," Lady Grant said, interrupting her thoughts as the carriage drew up to the house. "Oh, and at Lord Blackmore's ball tomorrow evening, everyone will be talking of it, I am sure! You shall have every eye on you, and will not need to hide at the back of the room any longer. You are to be his bride, Rachael! You are no longer a wallflower!"

Forcing a smile, Rachael climbed out of the carriage and walked to the house, suddenly aware of just how little she desired such a thing. The thought of being in the ballroom with every member of the *ton* watching her, aware of her presence, sent such a coldness down her spine; she shivered violently as she hurried inside. How strange it was that now, at the time when she ought to be rejoicing that she would not be seen as a wallflower any longer, that was the only thing – and the only place – she wished to be?

"BETROTHED?" Lady Frederica's eyes widened, her expression of astonishment matching both Lady Alice's and Mis Fairley's. "You are *betrothed*?"

"I am. And no doubt you will hear of it all very soon," Rachael replied, looking down at her hands. "The *ton* are sure to be speaking of it this evening and, though I have no intention of stepping out of this house again until the ball tomorrow, I can already practically hear my name on the lips of everyone in society!" With a wry smile, she glanced at each of her friends in turn and saw the shock written on every face. The only one absent was Miss Bosworth, though Rachael had been very well able to forgive her the absence given all that she was enduring at present.

"Goodness." Lady Alice shook her head and then offered Rachael a smile. "I do hope you are a little pleased, despite the circumstances of your betrothal being a little... unexpected!"

Rachael managed to smile, though her heart was still somewhere between confusion and happiness.

"I am still a little overwhelmed by it all. I have gone this morning from being a young lady without connection, to someone who will now be married come the end of the Season!" Even saying that aloud made her feel a little dizzy, and she sat back in her chair, one hand going to her forehead as she closed her eyes, not at all concerned with propriety. She wanted to be true, to be honest to her friends about her present circumstances and her feelings, and hiding it would do no good. "Goodness, I am a little overcome, I think!"

"As we can all understand." Miss Fairley smiled warmly.

"But what about all these rumors?" Lady Alice asked as Rachael opened her eyes, reaching for her cup of tea which sat to one side of her on a small side table. "Are you just to forget about them all?"

Rachael took in a breath and considered.

"I had not thought about that. I am not certain what

ought to be done. Either we do forget them and leave things as they are, or we continue to seek out the truth." Her shoulders lifted and then fell. "There has been no further attempt to spread gossip about him. Perhaps whoever wished to do such a thing – for whatever reason – has given up."

"Though I think you should still tell Lord Blackmore about the conversation you heard between the two ladies," Lady Frederica put in, as Rachael nodded. "I presume you have not had the opportunity to do so as yet?"

Rachael smiled ruefully.

"No, not as yet. I did say to him, upon our parting, that I wanted to speak with him about this and, indeed, was about to commence with a conversation only to see one gentleman and two ladies hurrying towards us and, given that they would, no doubt, have wanted to speak to us about the betrothal, I took my leave. It will wait for another time." A small smile crept up one side of her mouth. "Perhaps the danger has passed. The *ton* will be so busy speaking of our betrothal, that even if there was another rumor spread, it might fade away to nothing."

"Do be cautious."

A gentle frown caught Rachael's forehead.

"You think it might still be a concern, Miss Fairley?"

"I do," came the reply. "I would like to agree with you but to my mind, after hearing the conversation from the two ladies, and being aware of what has been said before, I would urge caution. It might be an excellent opportunity for whoever this is to say something more, to speak even more ill, though I still cannot comprehend what their purpose in doing so might be."

Rachael considered this and, seeing her friend's wisdom, thanked her for it.

"Someone is clearly eager to bring Lord Blackmore low," Lady Frederica put in, quietly. "They wish to ruin his reputation, to have him unworthy of society's consideration. Firstly, last Season, they sought to have him seen as a rogue, a gentleman who would have young ladies at his townhouse late in the evening and into the following morning. Why your name was attached to it, Miss Simmons, might simply have been the choice of whoever is behind this, merely because they needed a young lady of quality who could be attached to the situation to make Lord Blackmore appear all the more a scoundrel."

Rachael scowled.

"Which does not speak very highly of them. Clearly, they did not consider what would happen to my reputation."

"I doubt they think of anything save for themselves." Miss Fairley clicked her tongue in displeasure as Lady Alice nodded. "Their purpose is to stand against Lord Blackmore, regardless of whoever else they must use to gain what they want."

"I cannot think of who it might be, and Lord Blackmore assures me that he has no enemies." A troubling thought pinched at Rachael's mind, and she let out a breath, her brows furrowing. "I do worry now, that, when the time comes for me to marry Lord Blackmore, there will be this weight, this shadow which will cover us, which will *cling* to us. We will not know who it is who has done this, who has spread the rumors, and whether or not they will seek to do so again. That is a worry which will linger, I fear."

Lady Alice smiled gently, chasing away some of Rachael's worry.

"Or it may fade, if nothing more comes of it," she suggested, countering Rachael's concerns. "You may find yourself so happy that you forget about it entirely, and nothing but joy and contentment will be yours."

Seeing the smiling faces of her friends, Rachael clasped her hands lightly in her lap and smiled back at them, letting her happiness begin to grow as she thought about soon becoming Lady Blackmore. There was a lot for them to discuss, yes, and she still had her own heart to contend with, but now that she had been allowed to think on it, to let the realization of what her future would be settled in upon her mind, Rachael had to admit one thing.

It was nothing short of wonderful.

CHAPTER ELEVEN

"My hearty congratulations, old boy!"

Hugh smiled and shook Lord Elmsford's hand.

"It is good to see you here this evening."

"You did not think that I would miss this wonderful occasion, did you?" Lord Elmsford grinned as he released Hugh's hand. "And yes, Lord Kelling has informed me of everything. We must talk later this evening, though I will say that I am pleased to hear of your betrothal. I think it is a magnificent idea."

"You do?"

Lord Elmsford chuckled as he walked away.

"Of course I do. I think I even suggested it some time ago! Come and find me later this evening, once you have greeted all of your guests."

Hugh smiled and promised that he would, ready then to greet his next guest in the welcoming line. This evening, thus far, had been a success, given that those he had invited had all come to attend his ball, rather than rejecting it for fear they would be standing in the ballroom with a pauper who had been unable to match their expectations. Some, he was certain, had come out of nothing more than curiosity, wanting to see whether he would truly be able to throw a spectacular ball, and Hugh was silently pleased to see their wide eyes and hear their excited exclamations. He had spent a great deal on decorating the ballroom, so there were now silk drapes pulled into long loops along the walls themselves, interspersed with fresh flowers and cuts of ivy. The orchestra was the very finest London could produce and the champagne was the very best – and certainly would not be watered down! This was a chance to show the *ton* that he was not without coin, and he was certainly not in fear of lacking wealth and Hugh had given a great deal of money to it.

He was certainly proving his point.

"Good evening, Lord Blackmore."

Hugh inclined his head.

"Lady Hastings, good evening."

The lady's lip curled.

"Is it true that you have thrown yourself away on a young lady unworthy of you, Lord Blackmore?"

A little surprised at the direct comment, given that a simple greeting was all that was required at this juncture, Hugh paused for a moment, wondering if Lady Hastings would move away, but she did not. Instead, she glared at him as though he had done something wrong, leaving him both confused and uncertain.

"I am betrothed to a very worthy young lady, Lady

Hastings, I thank you." Keeping his tone cool and his words a little clipped, Hugh lifted his eyebrows and gazed back at the lady resolutely, refusing to be cowed. "It is a great disappointment when members of the *ton* are inclined towards listening to gossip and continuing to cling to it, even when it is proven, beyond all doubt, that there is no responsibility to be borne by the person in question."

Lady Hastings clicked her tongue.

"You are an *Earl,* Lord Blackmore," she said, as though Hugh was somehow unaware of this. "You ought to be marrying a young lady of quality, one who is of the same status in terms of her breeding as you are. Miss Simmons is only the daughter of a Viscount and, given what is currently clinging to her, is certainly not the right choice when it comes to being your bride."

Hugh frowned.

"I also have rumors clinging to my name, Lady Hastings. Some believe I am a scoundrel and a rogue. That was the whisper from last Season and this Season - I am meant to be an impoverished fellow, someone who cannot keep a bit of coin in his hand, given my debt to some gambling den or other."

To his surprise, Lady Hastings only laughed and waved a hand.

"My dear Lord Blackmore, it is foolish to even *suggest* that those whispers are true! Your character is well known, and it is now said that it must simply have been an error in observation on the part of whoever watched Miss Simmons... or whoever it was, removing themselves from that townhouse." Her face flushed, but her eyes remained steady. "And as for the lie that you are impoverished, all one need do is look at this ball! It is quite clear to me that you have more than enough coin to pay for all of this and, therefore, I do not believe a word of that rumor either. Therefore, Lord Blackmore, as I have said, it is not a wise match for you. You would be far better to consider someone who is of the same standing as you, and who does not have even a single piece of gossip attached to their name." Her eyes slid left and with a smile, she inclined her head. "Good evening, Lord Blackmore."

"Good evening."

Frowning, Hugh turned to Lady Tabitha who had been waiting patiently beside her mother for some minutes. She was pink-cheeked, a smile on her face, and her eyes held fast to his, just as her mother's had done. A heavy weight dropped into Hugh's stomach as he bowed over her hand and murmured a greeting, though he was relieved when she hurried after her mother almost at once rather than lingering in conversation.

Was Lady Hastings trying to suggest that her own daughter might be a good match for him? A shudder passed through his frame, and he threw the thought away almost as quickly as it had come, turning to greet the next guest with as much of a smile as he could muster. And, as he did so, all that he found within him was a great and desperate longing for Miss Simmons' company. There was so much for them to say to each other and, in truth, he did not even know how she felt about their betrothal. It was *she* he wanted to speak with, only her company that he desired, and with desperate, searching eyes, he gazed down the line of guests waiting to greet him, only to be disappointed.

Miss Simmons was not there.

"Good evening, Lord Blackmore."

Rather tired from the long, exhausting requirement to greet every guest, Hugh went to smile a little dispassionately at whoever it was greeting him now, only for his eyes to flare and his heart to leap so fervently, he was forced to catch his breath.

"Miss Simmons!"

"I do hope that you will forgive me for being tardy," she said, as Lady Grant hovered a few steps behind her. "The truth is, I was aware that a good many people would wish to speak with me, and I wanted to avoid being the center of everyone's attention for as long as I could. I thought that once the ball was well underway, the rest of the guests might not pay me as much attention." Her smile twinkled up into her eyes. "I am glad to say that I have been proven correct, thus far."

"I am relieved for you." Hugh offered her a slightly wry smile. "I have had many a person seek me out to ask me about something or another related to our betrothal." His smile fell away as her gaze tugged from his. "We have not spoken of it together, I know, but at the moment, I did wonder if–"

"I have no intention of refusing or begging to end our betrothal," she interrupted quietly, making his breath rush out of him in one long sound. "I am quite agreed that we shall wed. Though I have some things I should like to discuss with you."

"Of course, of course." Putting one hand to his heart, Hugh closed his eyes briefly and smiled. "I will speak to your father also. I must apologize to him for not going about this the correct way."

Miss Simmons laughed, and Hugh grinned, the sound delighting his heart.

"I can assure you, my father will do nothing other than thank you, as I ought to do," came the reply, though her face began to flush gently as she looked up at him. "It was unexpected, certainly – for us both, I think – but you have offered me something that I had begun to fear I would never be able to have. Instead of seeing the future as nothing but darkness and solitude, I have it now filled with light and companionship. That is truly wonderful."

When she reached out and touched his hand with hers, when her fingers caught his and held there, something so profound occurred, Hugh could neither speak nor move. It was as if he had stepped into the sunshine, but sunshine such as he had never known before. It was brighter, warmer, and more pleasant than anything he had ever experienced, and the joy of it completely stole away every part of his senses. His breath swirled in his chest, his blood thundered in his veins, and as his fingers tightened around hers, the rush of desire to pull her into his arms became so strong that he had to curl his toes in his boots to prevent himself from doing so.

"I am glad that we are betrothed." The voice from his throat sounded gruff, thick, and entirely unlike him, making him flush with embarrassment. "What was it that you wished to discuss with me, might I ask?"

Miss Simmons pulled her hand from his and an instant chill flew through Hugh's veins, leaving him suddenly cold.

"There was something which I wished to tell you. It was only a few days ago when I attended a soiree. I was, of course, at the back of the room, and overheard a conversation which has had me a little perplexed."

"Oh?" Hoping his voice had returned to normal, Hugh tilted his head. "What do you mean?"

Miss Simmons frowned, her gaze drawing away from his again.

"It was a little strange. Either their conversation meant nothing at all, *or* it meant so much that it is very significant indeed, and might, in the end, lead us – or you – to whoever it is who has been speaking of you so badly."

Hugh's eyebrows lifted, surprise filling his chest.

"Is that so? Might you be willing to tell me what you overheard?"

She smiled at him.

"I should be glad to. It seems as though there is the occasional advantage to being a wallflower!"

"Lord Blackmore!"

Turning his head, and a little frustrated by the interruption, Hugh scowled at Lord Elmsford.

"Must you interrupt me now?" he asked, half-teasingly. "Can you not see that I am speaking with my betrothed?"

"I can, but I must speak with you first. It is urgent."

Hugh looked into his friend's face, seeing the gravity

settling into the man's expression and, instantly, his stomach dropped as his heart clenched hard.

"I can speak with you both, if you wish it?" Lord Elmsford asked, looking at Miss Simmons. "Since you are now betrothed, it might be best if this occurred."

"Yes, I quite agree." Hugh reached for Miss Simmons' hand. "Come, let us go to the parlor."

He did not hesitate, did not stop to ask if Lady Grant ought to join them, for such was his worry, he wished to make his way there without hesitation. Thankfully, Miss Simmons did not make a complaint either, and striding through the crowd, Hugh led the way to the main door of the ballroom and walked along the hallway with quick steps until they could step into the parlor.

"What is it?" he demanded, having loosened his grip on Miss Simmons' hand, though not released it entirely. "Have you heard something new?"

"I have." Lord Elmsford pushed one hand through his hair and began to pace up and down the small parlor, his expression grave, but his eyes darting from one thing to the next. "It was quite by chance, though I fear that this rumor may be the very worst of them all."

A knot tied itself into Hugh's stomach.

"Worse than being considered a rogue and then impoverished?"

Lord Elmsford nodded, and turned on his heel, moving back up the room towards Hugh.

"I heard the whisper given to me that you are not the rightful heir to the title."

"What?" Shock had an exclamation flying from Hugh's mouth as Lord Elmsford nodded, but did not look at him, continuing his pacing. "They think I ought not to be the Earl of Blackmore?"

"Precisely."

"For what reason?"

Scrubbing one hand down his face, Lord Elmsford took in a long breath and then huffed it out before coming to a complete stop.

"Because," he said, his voice low, "they are whispering that you are illegitimate."

Hugh stared at his friend, but Lord Elmsford only nodded miserably.

"Who is saying such a thing?" Miss Simmons whispered, one hand at her throat, her eyes wide and staring. "Who would dare suggest-?"

"I do not know."

Hugh swallowed hard, then dropped his head as he let out a heavy breath. There was nothing that he could say in answer to this, nothing that he could do to prove that he *was* the legitimate son of his late father and mother.

"That is a strong rumor to place upon my shoulders. Someone must have a great deal of audacity to say such a thing as that of me."

"Indeed." Lord Elmsford shook his head. "I cannot imagine who would have the gall to say it – but what troubles me the most is that there are those who will believe it, those who will be content to *repeat* it, and those who will continue to hold such an idea tight to their minds. Some may even give you the cut direct."

"I must find out who is responsible." A buzzing began to go around and around in his head as he fought to remain steady, to try to find a way to discover who it was that was speaking such dark things of him. "This cannot be allowed to continue." Turning, he looked down into Miss Simmons' eyes, a heaviness within his heart as he saw tears glistening there. "Miss Simmons – Rachael, if you wish, you may separate yourself from me. I do not want you to feel as though you must linger by my side. Yes, we have said that we are betrothed, but this rumor is so very significant, that it could damage you a great deal. If you wish it, we can separate, we can put an end to this betrothal, and no one would think less of you for doing so. After all, someone who is considered illegitimate by the *ton* will forever have questions about their family and their name." Ignoring the cry of his heart, a cry which demanded that he retract all he had just said, and cling to Miss Simmons, Hugh squeezed her fingers gently. "If you wish it, Miss Simmons, I will release you and take full responsibility for it. After all, it was my haste which had us betrothed in the first place!"

Miss Simmons searched his expression, her eyes still gleaming with gentle tears. She did not speak for some time and when she did, it came with a slow, shuddering breath.

"No, Blackmore." Swallowing his surprise, Hugh let out something between a huff and a gasp of relief, his fingers tightening on hers again. "No, I will not have you step away from me." Smiling, she lifted her free hand and pressed it to his cheek, sending fire rippling down through him. "Nor shall I step back from you. We are betrothed, are we not? And that means that we shall face whatever it is that comes next. You were willing to do what you could for me, when the rumors from last Season still clung to me, were you not?" Her fingers trailed down his neck, to his shoulder and then fell to her side. "What sort of person would I be if I stepped back from you now? No, Lord Blackmore, I will not end our betrothal. I will not be afraid of what is to come. Rather, I will stand beside you and show society that we do not accept this rumor, that we are not in the least bit afraid of what might be said." Her smile began to grow, her eyes brightening, and, with that came a confidence within Hugh himself that tore down the wall that fear had built up within him. "We shall succeed, Lord Blackmore. I am certain of it."

Hugh smiled at her and, after a moment, looked to Lord Elmsford.

"It seems that we are to continue as we are," he said, seeing his friend nod, though he did not smile. "Come now, let us return to the ball so that I might dance with my betrothed." Turning his head, he lifted Miss Simmons' hand and pressed a kiss to it before looking back into her eyes, seeing the gentle flush of her cheeks and the softness of her expression. "Should you like to waltz, my dear Miss Simmons?"

"Yes, Blackmore," came the whispered reply. "I should like to waltz in your arms again very much. I do not think I have known a happiness like it since the first time we stepped out together."

"Then I will do my utmost to make it all the more wonderful," he promised, before settling her hand on his arm and turning towards the door. Taking a breath, he made his way back to the ballroom, Miss Simmons on his arm and his head held high. He was not about to lose her, was not about to have her step away from him and that brought him more relief than he was able to express.

All he had to do now was survive this devastating rumor - and quite how he was to go about that, Hugh had very little idea.

CHAPTER TWELVE

Rachael's shoulders dropped as her father cleared his throat gruffly.

"A very bad business." Setting the paper down, he looked keenly across the table towards her. "I do not believe a word of it, of course."

"Thank you, Father." With a small smile, Rachael looked to her mother who reached across to squeeze her hand. "I am disappointed that it has made its way into the society pages. Something like that ought to be ignored, ought to be pushed aside, given the severity of the rumor."

"I quite agree, but society feeds upon gossip as though it is a starving animal, and something like this will satisfy it for some days," her father replied, giving her a sympathetic smile in return. "But you will be happy nonetheless, I am sure."

"Of that, you can be quite certain." Speaking with a little more firmness, Rachael took a deep breath. "I am looking forward to the day I shall marry."

Lady Grant smiled.

"I am glad to hear you say such a thing, my dear. I do think that Lord Blackmore is an excellent fellow, despite what is said of him."

Lord Grant coughed and then shook his head.

"It seems to me as though there is something – or someone – doing their utmost to ruin him. This is the third or fourth rumor which concerns him, is it not?"

Rachael held her father's gaze, relieved that he too could see the strangeness of all that had been thrown at Lord Blackmore.

"It is. Last Season, I believe, someone sought to ruin his good name and brought my own into the rumor also – though quite why *I* was chosen, I do not know! Lord Blackmore originally planned to stay at his estate for this Season, but was brought back to London by a friend, who encouraged him to linger for a short while. Within only a few days of his return, however, it seems as though this person, whoever they are, decided once more to spread a rumor about him which might have sent a weaker man scurrying back to their estate!"

Lord Grant nodded and rubbed one hand over his chin.

"It is all rather strange. Why would someone wish him to return to his estate? Why would they wish him to be ruined in the eyes of society, even though he has never done anything worthy of such censure?" His hand went back to the table. "It seems to me that Lord Blackmore has an enemy, and my advice to you, my dear, is to discover the identity of this person before you wed. Not because I believe that you ought not to marry him, but because it would be wise to understand this situation fully before you become his bride."

"He is doing his best, Father." Rachael offered a small, sad smile. "But if nothing should change between now and the day of our wedding, I will still stand up and take my place beside him. I want nothing more."

"I quite understand," her mother answered her, softly, as Rachael's heart swelled with even the mere thought of standing up to make her promises to Lord Blackmore. "You have found a good husband, Rachael, and we are both very happy for you."

Rachael smiled and picked up her teacup, her happiness growing despite the circumstances they had been discussing. When she and Lord Blackmore had spoken to Lord Elmsford at the ball, she had felt the connection between herself and Lord Blackmore increasing in strength, and when he had taken her hand and gazed deeply into her eyes, she had wanted nothing more than to pull herself into him, to feel his arms encircle her waist and to breathe in the very essence of him.

Of course, she had done no such thing, and that had come with a sense of regret, though it had not been at all the most appropriate moment for such a display of her feelings. All the same, that desire lingered within her still, and she found her smile growing steadily, as she wondered when she might have the opportunity to give in to all that she desired… and if she would have enough boldness to do so.

"The bookshop?"

Rachael smiled.

"Very well, though I do not think that books are part of my trousseau."

Her mother laughed, and Rachael's smile grew all the more, as she found herself more than a little contented, given how wonderful an afternoon they had been enjoying. Purchasing things for her trousseau, discussing the wedding itself, and what it would be like to be mistress of the Earl's estate, was making Rachael's anticipation and excitement grow with a furious strength and, even though the shadow of these latest rumors hung over her, she was able to push them back far enough to almost forget them entirely.

"Very well, shall we see if you need any new ribbons?"

Gesturing to another shop, Lady Grant smiled as Rachael nodded and together, arm in arm, mother and daughter walked into the shop.

It was rather quiet, which was a little surprising for that time of day, but Rachael thought it something of a relief, given the fact that she might have garnered one or two sidelong looks and whispers within the shop otherwise. She and her mother moved about the shop independently, with her mother quickly engaging the shopkeeper in conversation about lace, ribbon, and the like, leaving Rachael free to look around.

The door behind her opened, the bell tinkling as two ladies stepped inside. After glancing over her shoulder, Rachael went to look away again, only to pause and stare, wide-eyed, at the second of the two ladies.

She recognized her.

"I will not be long!" the first lady said, giving the second a warm smile which was not returned. "Why must you look so downhearted? It is not as though I have taken an age in every shop we have stepped into, is it?"

The second lady rolled her eyes and folded her arms, giving a huff that was clearly meant to indicate that she felt as though she were giving a great deal of her time and effort to whatever endeavor the first lady was engaged in. Tossing her head, her blonde curls bouncing, she heaved another sigh, but despite her actions, the first lady made no effort to hurry. Rachael turned her head away again, not wishing to be caught staring, but searched her mind for who this lady was. Why did she recognize her? And why was her attitude itself so familiar?

"*Do* hurry up."

The slightly whining tones wrapped themselves around Rachael's mind, and she frowned hard, rubbing one hand over her forehead as she thought.

It came to her with such swiftness, she snatched in a breath, her eyes flaring wide.

I know who it is.

The second lady was the one whom she had overheard discussing Lord Blackmore. The one who had been so very rude to her when she had walked into her path, the one who had offered no smile, no look of interest or the like but nothing other than frustration and anger.

Her eyes closed. *I was meant to tell Lord Blackmore of this. And yet again, I have not.*

Frustration rose within her and she scowled, her jaw tightening at her foolishness. She was meant to have told him, long before now, about the conversation she had overheard and seeing this lady again had only served to remind her that she had not managed to do that as yet.

Her eyes flew open. Mayhap she could find a way to discover this lady's name. After all, would it not be better if she could speak with Lord Blackmore and inform him as to who one of the ladies was, at the very least?

Resolved, Rachael looked about the shop and spotted the first lady who was now looking through a stack of ribbons. Putting a smile on her face, she meandered over in her direction, throwing only the occasional glance over her shoulder to make sure that the second lady was a little further away from them and would not hear Rachael's conversation.

"Your friend is not interested in ribbons, mayhap?"

The first lady looked up at Rachael from where she had been bent over the ribbons, only to smile.

"Not at the moment, at least!"

Glad that there had been a warmth in the lady's response rather than a rude coldness, Rachael smiled at her.

"Might I be able to help you? I am also seeking a new ribbon, and there are so many here... Together we may be quicker sifting through them. Your friend appears to be in something of a rush and perhaps–"

The lady nodded, smiling again.

"Emily... that is to say, Lady Alderton, is eager for me to choose my ribbons simply so that we might make our way to the shop that *she* wishes to attend," came the reply, making Rachael's smile a little fixed. "However, I will accept your help so that her frown might not linger too long, else her mood will become all the worse!"

Rachael moved closer and helped the lady find the length and color of ribbon that she desired, though she did not once ask the lady for her own title. With a smile of delight, the lady took the ribbon she had chosen and made to step away, only to smile at Rachael.

"Thank you for your help, Miss....?"

"It was my pleasure," Rachael replied, making certain not to give her title. "I think I shall beg my mother to purchase me the green satin, for I believe that it will suit me very well! Good afternoon."

The young lady did not appear to notice that Rachael had not given her either her name or title and, with a smile and another murmur of thanks, walked back across to where the shopkeeper stood. Turning her back so that the second lady would not see her, Rachael waited until she heard the doorbell ring again as the two ladies departed, and without wasting a moment, she hurried back across the shop to where her mother stood.

"I must go to visit Lord Blackmore."

Lady Grant frowned.

"At this very moment? We do not know if he will be at home, Rachael."

"I understand that, Mama, but I must go to call upon him at once. It is of the greatest urgency."

Much to her relief, her mother did not question her further. Instead, she only nodded and, with a smile and a promise to the shopkeeper to return at their earliest opportunity, both she and Rachael walked out of the shop.

"Rachael! Good afternoon!"

Rachael blinked, then swallowed hard as Lady Alice came to join them, accompanied by Lady Frederica.

"Good day, Lady Alice, Lady Frederica. I am so very sorry, but I must go at once to call on Lord Blackmore."

Lady Frederica frowned.

"Is this about the rumors?"

With a shake of her head, Rachael glanced at her mother – who had stepped away – and then spoke in low tones.

"I have only just seen one of the two ladies whom I overheard at the soiree. What is more, I have discovered the title of one of them."

Both of her friends' eyebrows lifted at once and Rachael managed a small smile despite the sense of urgency pushing her to hurry and take her leave of her friends.

"And you have not spoken to Lord Blackmore about them as yet?" In answer to Lady Alice's question, Rachael shook her head no. "Then you will be glad to know that I believe I have just seen him step into the bookshop," Lady Alice continued, with a small smile as Rachael caught her breath and turned around sharply.

Her hand went to Lady Alice's, grasping it tightly as she nodded in the direction of the bookshop.

"And there, those two ladies are making their way inside also," she whispered, her heart suddenly in her throat. "What do you think they will be doing?"

"I think they will be looking for a book," Lady Frederica replied, calmly. "Come now, they will not know that he has gone in there, I am sure of it. Why do we not all go in together?"

Rachael nodded and, seeing her mother talking to an acquaintance, quickly told her that she was going to the bookshop with her friends and would return presently. Whether this confused Lady Grant, given Rachael's previous eagerness to make her way to Lord Blackmore's residence, Rachael did not know or care. All that mattered now was finding Lord Blackmore, and making certain that he was safe from whatever dark plans Lady Alderton had in mind for him.

CHAPTER THIRTEEN

"*L*ord Blackmore!"

Hugh turned around, only to smile as Miss Simmons hurried towards him, an urgency in her steps which he hoped came from an eagerness to be in his company.

"Rachael... I mean, Miss Simmons." Seeing two of her friends coming behind her, he quickly reverted to formality. "How pleasant to see you. I do hope that you are well?" Seeing the whiteness of her cheeks, he frowned. "I am sorry if this latest rumor has done you harm. I have been doing what I can to behave just as usual, though I have noticed a significant amount of sharp glances being given to me."

She shook her head, her hand finding his and grasping it tightly.

"We must speak at once. I should have told you of this some days ago, but with everything that has happened, I have struggled to find the time to do so."

Hugh's frown grew.

"Of course. What is it that you wish to speak of?"

"Not here," Miss Simmons murmured, looking around and nodding to her two friends, who both immediately turned and began to meander around the bookshop, though they did not move too far from where he and Miss Simmons stood. "Come with me, if you would. A little further into the shop will suffice."

Despite the clear tension humming through the air, Hugh could not help the kick of excitement that came as she led him in between bookcases and down to what seemed to be the very depths of the shop. Aged books lined the bookshelves, and there was certainly a lot more dust than in the front part of the shop. They certainly were tucked away, but he must be careful not to disturb the dust, lest they sneeze!

Whatever it was that Miss Simmons wanted to say, it was important enough to require that they remain as hidden as possible. Hugh's stomach tightened as she looked up into his face and then took both of his hands in hers.

"I have no intention of ending our betrothal or the like, if that is what the worry etched across your face is about." Miss Simmons smiled briefly, though her gaze remained steady. "As I said, I should have spoken to you of this previously, but with everything that has happened, I quite forgot."

"Then tell me now," he said, softly. "What is it that burdens you?"

Miss Simmons closed her eyes and took in a breath.

"It is concerning a conversation I overheard some

time ago, as a wallflower. It was between two ladies, and they spoke of you."

Hugh's shoulders dropped.

"Another rumor?"

"No, it was not that," Miss Simmons reassured him, though she did frown. "It was a conversation which I could not fully understand. Two ladies spoke of you, and the situation which had almost occurred with Lady Duthell. One stated that it was most unfortunate, though I could not be certain as to whether she meant it was unfortunate that you should be caught up in such a thing or that it was unfortunate that you had avoided it."

Hugh's heart squeezed.

"I see."

"I should have told you about this before now, though mayhap it means nothing," Miss Simmons continued, her eyes dropping to the floor for a moment. "However, it was on seeing the second lady today – the one who, I believe, was speaking of you in such a way, that I realized it was something I ought to have told you long before now. I am sorry I did not."

"Please." Releasing one of her hands, Hugh set it to her chin and gently lifted it, so that she looked up into his eyes. "This is not something which you need to apologize for. It is quite understandable, given that so much has taken place! Thank you for telling me now."

Miss Simmons' worried expression softened and, before he knew what he was doing, Hugh found himself leaning down, the desire to kiss her beginning to grow like a sudden fire sweeping right through him. It was only when Miss Simmons' eyes flared in surprise that he stopped himself, swallowing hard and looking away as he dropped his hand to his side and stood up straight.

"Forgive me." Clearing his throat gruffly, he struggled to look back into her eyes for fear of embarrassing himself further. "I did not mean—"

"I was only a little astonished." Miss Simmons' hand squeezed his as she spoke softly, and Hugh finally brought his gaze back to hers. "It is not as though..." Her face flushed, but she smiled, still looking up at him. "I confess that my heart feels an abundance of emotions, Lord Blackmore. It pulls from one to another without any warning but, in the midst of it all, is the awareness that I have a great and growing affection for you. Despite all of the rumors, the difficulties, and the strain which has come with our present circumstances, that affection continues to grow, and that is something which I find myself to be very happy about indeed."

Hugh did not wait another moment. To hear that her heart sang with an affection for him, much as his own did for her, was too much for him to hear without acting upon it. Putting his arms around her waist, he lowered his head again, taking his time and moving with a great slowness so as not to overwhelm her. Miss Simmons did not hesitate, however. She lifted her chin, closed her eyes, and waited for him to close the distance – and Hugh did so at once.

Their kiss was soft and sweet, the gentleness of her mouth against his sending heat streaking down to his core. Her hands moved slowly up his chest to around his neck, her fingers pushing into his hair as he angled his head just a little. Her hands tightened and Hugh pulled her all the closer, his heart singing for the sheer joy that came with this moment. It was not something which he would ever forget and, as their kiss finally broke apart, Hugh took in a ragged breath, a little surprised at how overcome he was by the simplest of kisses.

"I must hope, Blackmore, that there is something in your heart for me also." Miss Simmons' cheeks burned hot, but her eyes searched his face, a clear urgency in them. "I thought that... I had a little hope that there was even the smallest–"

Hugh caught her lips with his again, silencing her concerns and sweeping them away as he held her close. She sighed as he set himself apart from her again, though he kept his forehead resting gently against hers.

"Yes, Rachael. I will admit to you openly that my heart holds a strong affection for you in return. I only wish that I had been bold enough to speak of it before you, so you might have had the assurance of the return of your affections!" Smiling gently, he cupped her face in his hands, looking down into her shining eyes. "I am astounded by your beauty, by your strength, and your courage. Your willingness to linger by my side, to hold fast to our betrothal, when many a young woman might have stepped away, makes me all the more grateful for you. I did not ever imagine that I would be stepping into marriage with someone who holds my heart as you do, but now that such a thing has been offered me, it is something which I am all the more grateful for."

Miss Simmons sighed contentedly and closed her eyes.

"It feels as though nothing else in the world matters

aside from my standing here with you," she said softly, as Hugh found his heart understanding entirely what she meant. "Everything that has concerned me, everything that I have pulled back from, it all seems to be so very little now." Her eyes opened "Even Lady Alderton's remarks—"

"Lady Alderton?" Hugh's smile dropped, his stomach twisting as he looked into Miss Simmons' eyes, seeing her frown growing in the place of her smile. "Did you say Lady Alderton?"

"Yes, I did." Miss Simmons took a step back from him, their tender moment gone. "Why?"

Heat ran over Hugh's skin, followed by a shuddering cold. Squeezing his eyes shut, he turned around completely, putting his head back and groaning aloud as he fought to find something to say.

"That name means something to you." Miss Simmons drew closer, one hand to his arm as she leaned in towards him again. "Oh, goodness, I should have said something sooner! The moment I saw her and heard what was said, I should have come to tell you at once."

Hugh shook his head.

"You are not to bear any guilt or blame in this. It is only now, on hearing the name that I realize there may be something significant here... though I cannot understand why it would be." Miss Simmons' frown remained, but she said nothing, thinking that the silence would encourage him to explain further, but he did not. There was too much on his mind. It must be too great a concern for him to share with her at present. "I will not say more yet, my dear lady. Is it not because I have no wish to, but rather because I wish to consider the matter a little more. I may be entirely wrong in all of my thinking, and it would not be right for me to discuss it with you at present, not until I am entirely certain."

Miss Simmons caught her lip between her teeth for a moment, then gestured to the front of the bookshop.

"Would it help if I were to inform you that Lady Alderton was present, here, at this very moment?"

Hugh's eyes flared.

"Within the bookshop?"

"Yes, I saw her enter before I came to join you. I was afraid that she might seek to do something more to you, while you remained entirely unawares. She is around my height, with brown eyes and fair curls."

"I am grateful to you for your concern. I do not know Lady Alderton, however." His spirits dipped for a moment only for him to rally them again. "But I thank you. There is much I must consider and act upon now if I am to find the truth." Looking back at her, he lifted his shoulders and then let them fall. "I may be mistaken, however. My thoughts might bear nothing of the truth, and it is for that reason that I remain cautious."

"I understand. If there is anything I can do to help you, then you need only ask."

"I am grateful to you for that." Lifting her hand, he pressed a kiss to the back of it before releasing it. "I must go." Pressing his lips tight together, he paused for a moment, then looked back at her again. "Did I ever tell you that I had a brother?"

Miss Simmons' eyes rounded.

"No, I do not think that you did."

Hugh nodded.

"My brother, Porter, Viscount Alderton, is in Bath at present. He married a short time ago and thus, that name makes me wonder if, somehow, he is connected to all of this, though I pray that I am wrong. I may take my leave of London and go to speak with him there, but should I depart, I will inform you before I leave."

He watched as, for a moment, a mixture of emotions ran wildly across her expression – confusion, worry, upset – only for her to smile, seemingly choosing not to ask him any further questions. Her trust in him was wonderful, and he pressed one hand to his heart, hoping that the gesture would speak to her in a way that he could not.

"Thank you."

Her smile grew.

"I will pray that you find the truth," she said, softly. "Goodbye, Blackmore."

Taking his leave, Hugh walked to the front of the bookshop, glancing to his left and, as he did so, saw a young lady with rather sharp features, fair hair, and narrowed brown eyes gazing back at him. There came no flicker of recognition, no awareness of the lady herself and, with a brief smile in her direction, Hugh stepped out of the shop and made his way back towards his carriage.

His steps grew quicker, his heart beginning to pound as he hurried to his carriage.

"To Lord Elmsford's townhouse," he called to his driver, who immediately nodded. "At once and with the greatest speed."

The driver was as good as Hugh knew him to be and

had the carriage pulling away the second the door was shut. It rattled quietly along the road, but Hugh's thoughts continued to trouble him, his head *and* heart heavy as he considered the possibility that someone close to him might have been the very person trying to ruin his life completely.

∽

"What do you mean, Lady Alderton?"

"Recall," Hugh said, a little impatiently, "I told you that my brother had married recently. I was not invited to the wedding, however. I was only informed of it through a very pretty letter that Lady Alderton sent to me, telling me how much she looked forward to our first meeting."

"And you have never met the lady."

Hugh shook his head no.

"And your brother is in Bath."

"As far as I am aware," Hugh exclaimed, throwing up his hands in frustration. "You do not appear to be listening to me, Elmsford! I do not care whether my brother is in Bath or not. What concerns me at present is the presence of this Lady Alderton here in London. I wonder if she is the wife of my brother and if it is as I believe, then I question what it is that she is doing here."

Lord Elmsford frowned.

"You believe that she may be the one behind all of these rumors."

"Worse. I fear that *he* is the one doing so, through her." Pain twisted his heart, and he took a steadying breath. "I do not say that simply because she is present in London, but because of what Miss Simmons overheard."

His friend's frown grew heavier.

"But for what purpose? What reason would your brother have to spread such rumors, and why would his bride be so willing?"

Hugh closed his eyes.

"I do not know," he said, letting out a slow breath as frustration began to build within him. "I have no answers. None. All I wish to do now is to find out the truth - and that means I must first go to Bath."

"To find your brother," Lord Elmsford put in, as Hugh nodded. "But what if he is not in Bath? What then?"

"I do not know!" Exclaiming furiously, Hugh threw up his hands and then shook his head, letting out a hiss of breath. "Forgive me, Elmsford, but I am lost and confused, and deeply, *deeply* concerned that what I fear will be proven true. At the same time, I find myself in love with Miss Simmons and want nothing more than to spend all of my time with her so that we might plan our wedding, but instead, I must resolve this! Believe me, it is not what I want to do, but what I must do."

Much to his surprise, Lord Elmsford did not appear to be in the least bit upset by this exclamation. Instead, he only chuckled and, walking across the room, poured himself a drink and then a measure for Hugh also.

"I am delighted to hear it." Handing him the glass, Lord Elmsford chinked his glass against Hugh's and then took a sip. He laughed aloud and slapped Hugh on the shoulder. "Despite your struggles, I am very glad indeed to hear that you have found such a happy match with Miss Simmons. How fortunate you are!"

Hugh took a breath and then let it out slowly, some of the tension fading from him as he thought about what Lord Elmsford had said.

"Yes," he agreed, after a few moments, "yes, I suppose I am very fortunate."

"Certainly, you are! It is not every gentleman who finds themselves with such affection! I presume that the lady returns it, given how happily she looks at you?" A slight flush crept up Hugh's neck as he nodded, though his friend only grinned. "Capital. Then you shall surely be very happy indeed, no matter what happens as regards your brother and his wife," Lord Elmsford declared, making Hugh's smile grow. "Is that not so?"

"It is," Hugh replied, his shoulders loosening and the remaining tension leaving him as he thought about the kiss he had shared with Miss Simmons, only an hour ago. "And that is what I shall think on, regardless of what I discover: the happiness which I have – and shall have – with the wonderful Miss Simmons."

CHAPTER FOURTEEN

*R*achael looked around the ballroom, her fingers twisting together as she sought out any sign of Lord Blackmore's presence. He had not yet left for Bath, though his note to her this afternoon said that he had every intention of making his way there by the end of the week, and thus he expected to be at the ball this evening.

"Standing there worrying will do nothing." Lady Frederica put one hand to her arm, and Rachael started, having quite forgotten that Lady Frederica was there. "He will come."

"I know. It is only that I fear what will be said." Rachael closed her eyes and tried to push her worries away, aware of what swept through her. "There is a great deal of gossip at present, over his current standing, and whether or not he truly *is* the Earl of Blackmore... and I dread hearing yet more whispers."

"And yet, they will come," Miss Fairley murmured,

sympathetically. "You will not be free of this yet - not until something is said – or done – that will either blow away all of the gossip and reveal it to be the chaff that it is, or something else is put in its place. While I hope it will be the first, I fear it will be the latter. However, that does not mean that you cannot continue to move through society, as we have all been trying to do. It is simply a matter of lifting one's chin a little higher and proving to the *ton,* as we have been attempting, that we will not be set back by their loose tongues and idle gossip."

Rachael nodded, though her heart continued to plague her with ongoing concerns.

"Look."

Rachael turned her head, just in time to see none other than Lady Alderton, accompanied by the lady she had seen with her when she had overheard their conversation about Lord Blackmore.

"Lord Blackmore must be informed that she is here. He still has not said anything to me, about what he knows of the lady or how she is in any way connected to him, but there was a deep worry in his eyes when I spoke her name."

As if the lady had overheard Rachael talking, she looked directly at her, and though Rachael swiftly tugged her gaze away, a white-hot heat ran straight through her, and she flushed.

"It may be nothing," Lady Frederica murmured, though she coughed quietly thereafter and nudged Rachael lightly. "Though it looks to me as though Lady Alderton is coming to speak with you."

The heat in her frame curled into her stomach, leaving Rachael feeling almost nauseated as she glanced again in Lady Alderton's direction, once more catching her gaze and then looking away.

"Why should she want to speak with me?"

It was a question that no one could answer, and within a moment, Lady Alderton had come to stand directly in front of Rachael, a challenge in her brown eyes.

"I hear that you are betrothed to Lord Blackmore."

Rachael blinked, having not expected this to be the first thing that the lady said to her.

"I beg your pardon?"

"You heard me, I am sure." Lady Alderton narrowed her eyes a fraction. "I said, you are betrothed to Lord Blackmore."

Rachael opened her mouth to confirm this to be true, only to see Miss Fairley standing just behind Lady Alderton, her expression one of frustration. Catching her friend's eye, Rachael saw how Miss Fairley shook her head and, taking that as a warning chose to give an entirely different response.

"Forgive me, but we are not acquainted. I am not at all inclined to answer questions from those I do not know."

Turning her head away, she shifted her whole body so that she was now at an angle, facing away from the lady, but she practically felt the instant anger radiating from Lady Alderton.

"How dare you? I am merely asking a question and you treat me with such disregard!"

Rachael threw her a quick glance and then smiled tightly.

"I do not answer questions from those I am not yet acquainted with. Quite how you know who I am, I cannot say but I certainly have not been introduced to you – and even if we were to be introduced and acquainted, I would still have every right to refuse to answer you. Good evening."

Lady Alderton, however, was not about to be ignored and, even as Rachael attempted to walk away, Lady Alderton stepped forward and moved directly into her path.

"You *will* listen to me," she hissed, one finger pointing directly at Rachael's chest. "I mean this to be a kindness, and yet you treat me with such disdain, I ought to keep what I have to warn you of to myself! It is just as you deserve."

Interest pricked up Rachael's ears, but she chose to remain steadfast, glad of the company of Lady Frederica, Miss Fairley, and standing a little further back, Lady Alice and Miss Bosworth, who were both watching the unfolding situation with careful eyes.

"You may keep your warnings entirely to yourself. I have no interest in them."

Lady Alderton took a step closer, her face red with anger over Rachael's refusal to listen.

"You are even more foolish than I imagined! Will you truly allow yourself to be placed in such a dark situation as to become Lord Blackmore's bride? You have a shame all of your own clinging to you, I well understand that, but there is no good reason for you to add to that."

Fire burned up Rachael's spine, heat behind her eyes.

"I have no shame whatsoever. I have nothing clinging to me, as you say. All that exists is whispers, none of which have any bearing upon my own standing."

Lady Alderton sneered, her hand dropping to her side.

"And yet, society does not believe that. They push you back to the shadows, for that is where they believe you belong. Will you now put yourself into an even darker situation? Any children you bear to Lord Blackmore will carry the same shame as their mother, and all because of your choice to marry the illegitimate heir to the Earl of Blackmore."

Rachael scrunched up her hands, her breathing coming in short, sharp gasps, such was her anger. Thankfully, seeing this, Lady Frederica stepped in at once.

"There is no truth to that rumor. There is no truth at all, and for you to speak it to Miss Simmons is designed only to bring her pain."

"I seek to warn her! Lord Blackmore is not as he seems, and I know that all too well."

"How can you know it?" Hearing that her voice sounded faint, Rachael closed her eyes briefly to steady herself. "There is no proof of that. There are only whispers." Opening her eyes again, she looked back into the face of Lady Alderton, disliking the way that the edge of her mouth twitched as though she were trying to hide a smile... or a sneer. "I will not take the word of a stranger over the promise of Lord Blackmore. And until there is proof of this, I will not believe a single part of it."

"Then you are even more foolish than I had at first thought."

Rachael took a small step closer.

"Insulting me will do nothing to encourage me to believe you," she said, quietly. "You are not known to me. You are nothing but a stranger who is, for whatever reason, seeking to break me apart from Lord Blackmore... unless, of course, that *is* your reason."

Her breath caught as she looked into the lady's face for a long moment, realizing, as she did so, that what she had suggested was entirely correct. That was the only thing that Lady Alderton was trying to do. She was doing her utmost to make certain that Rachael stepped away from Lord Blackmore, that their betrothal would come to an end, and he would be all the more injured in that.

Her breath caught as her anger reignited, seeing now exactly what it was that Lady Alderton wanted. She *was* responsible for all of the rumors and gossip surrounding Lord Blackmore, Rachael was sure of it, and in hoping to get Rachael to break off their betrothal, would be then able to spread yet more gossip about him.

But to what end?

"It was you."

The faint, half whisper came out of her lips without Rachael having intended to speak those words aloud, but Lady Alderton heard them, nonetheless.

"What are you talking about?"

Lady Alderton frowned, her hands going to her hips, but Rachael let out such a loud exclamation that her hands fell back to her sides and her eyes went wide.

"I *know* it was you!" Rachael cried, entirely unaware

of the small crowd that was gathering around her. "You are the one who has been spreading rumors and stories about Lord Blackmore. Is that not so? That is why you want me to end my betrothal to him so that you might take it and throw it across London in the hope of mortifying him all the more!"

The confidence that had been in Lady Alderton's face began to fade from her expression, though her eyes remained sharp.

"I do not know what you are talking about!"

"Yes, you do." Filled with a confidence that she had never experienced before, Rachael threw aside all caution, all worry and fear, and spoke so boldly, it seemed to silence the very music from the orchestra and, as she glanced around, made her quickly realize just how many of the *ton* were now watching.

I cannot falter now.

"You came to me in the hope that I would turn away from Lord Blackmore, did you not?" she said, clearly. "You have come to me with a rumor about his illegitimacy in the hope that it would be enough for me to remove myself from him. That way, you would be able to whisper more about him to the listening ear of the *ton* and, in doing so, bring him yet more suffering. Why else would you seek me out?"

Lady Alderton threw up her hands.

"Can not a lady of the *ton* show care and consideration for the young lady she sees to be a little too willing to step into the arms of a disgraced gentleman?"

"Except that you and I are not acquainted," Rachael replied, quickly, as Lady Alderton blinked and then looked away. "We have never been formally introduced. I have many friends who could speak to me about their concerns, and I would listen to them, of course. But you, someone I do not know, someone I have no acquaintance with, why would I then listen to you? It seems very strange that you would demand that I listen to you *and* that I act upon whatever you tell me, does it not?" Her head tilted. "What are your true motivations in this?"

"Yes, Lady Alderton!" cried someone from the gathered crowd. "Do tell us. Why would you accost this young lady in such a manner?"

"You said that you had proof of Lord Blackmore's illegitimacy," Lady Frederica added, as Lady Alderton began to go rather pale. "What is this proof?"

Lady Alderton's gaze flicked around the growing crowd, but Rachael kept her gaze steady. She was not about to let Lady Alderton escape from this, was not about to permit her to remove herself from this situation which she had brought upon herself, not without first offering Rachael some answers. Yes, Rachael might be considered a wallflower, but that did not mean that she was going to shrink back from this, to step back into the darkness which would then hide her from sight. She had the opportunity now to find the truth, and that meant holding her ground.

"You have been against Lord Blackmore from the very beginning," she said, softly. "Last Season, the rumor about my presence at his townhouse, might I ask if that came from your lips?"

"I – I did not know you then!" Lady Alderton

exclaimed, though her stammering came as evidence of her nervousness. "How could I have done such a thing?"

"You did not need to know me," Rachael replied, quickly. "All that was required was a name, and you gave it. It was just as others have suggested, an unfortunate circumstance where someone I was not acquainted with chose to use my name in their plan to pull Lord Blackmore low." She paused, waiting for Lady Alderton to say something or, at the very least, to deny what Rachael had said, but the lady chose to stay silent. Her gaze was no longer as sharp, her eyes no longer narrowed, and the confidence and assurance in her face and expression, which Rachael had seen so prominently, was now entirely absent. Was her silence a confirmation of her guilt?

"No doubt you hoped that the rumor from last Season, the one you had already perpetrated, would continue into this Season. Did you help it grow? Did you return to London and seek to push it further, in the hope that it would disgrace him all the more?" Again, Lady Alderton said nothing, and Rachael took a step closer, her hands tightening as she curled her fingers, tension and anticipation twining together within her. "And then, this Season, you have been determined to ruin him. You have attempted to set him in a position where, quite unexpectedly, he might have found himself in a circumstance not of his own making – I can see from the glimmer in your eyes that you know of what – and who – I am speaking – and thereafter, you sent around whispers that he is without coin. Alas, that failed also, given that he threw the most wonderful ball where it was quite clear that he has more than enough fortune! Your attempts have continued and yet, he has survived them all, refusing to give in, refusing to be cowed, and proving to society that these rumors are nothing more than idle whispers."

"And your very worst was to state that he is without legitimacy," Lady Alice put in, making Lady Alderton jump in surprise, given that Lady Alice stood behind her. "With his father and mother both passed away, there can be no one to easily prove otherwise. It is the very worst sort of rumor, for it can easily cling to the minds of those who have a willingness to believe it."

"Though I am not one who will do so," Rachael added, as her friends murmured the same. "I see this all for what it is, Lady Alderton. You, for whatever reason you might have to do so, have been persistently attacking Lord Blackmore in the hope of ruining him entirely, of sending him back from society and into his estate where he might live alone and slowly shrink away." Another thought wrapped itself around her heart, and she gasped, her eyes flaring wide. "Is that what you hoped for? For him to become so despondent that he might either give up his title by passing from this life much earlier than he might otherwise have done? To what end?"

There came a few gasps of shock from around the assembled group and Lady Alderton started violently, her eyes going wide as she looked all about the room.

"This is all quite ridiculous," she laughed, though the sound was tight and stretched thin. "You cannot suggest such things of me. I have no interest in Lord Blackmore, and would have no reason to do such a thing as that."

Rachael put her hands to her hips and looked Lady Alderton straight in the eye.

"You say that you have no interest in Lord Blackmore, and that you have no reason to do such things as I have put to you. But is it not true that you are married to Lord Blackmore's younger brother?"

There came ripples of shock as many of the onlookers gasped in surprise and then immediately began to whisper to each other, drawing the attention of Lady Alderton. Her eyes darted around the room and then back to Rachael, though there was nothing she could say, Rachael considered, which would make this situation any better for her.

"Yes, I *am* wed to that fool, Viscount Alderton." Keeping her voice low, Lady Alderton advanced towards Rachael, her face tight with either embarrassment or anger, Rachael could not tell which. "But he has no ambition, no desire for anything. Can you imagine what such a life is like? To discover that your husband is a gentleman who cares for nothing other than himself, and whatever it is that *he* desires? No, I have better ambitions than he."

"And thus, unsatisfied with your lot, you chose to try to push Lord Blackmore out of society, to ruin his name so that you and your husband might then take his place in society." Rachael's jaw tightened, seeing the flash in Lady Alderton's eyes. "What were you hoping for? To drive him to be a man so disgraced, so low in spirit that he would be easily convinced to give up his title by killing himself? So that your husband would take it in his place?"

"And what if I *did?*" Lady Alderton exclaimed, seeming now to lose control of her words and her actions, given the way that she flung up her hands and began to speak with such loud tones that everyone was certain to be able to hear her. "We married in haste, and I did not realize at the time that my husband bore only a courtesy title, while his elder brother held the title of Earl. You can imagine my disappointment, particularly when Lord Alderton appeared to behave just as any oaf might!"

"And thus, you attempted to come up with a way to gain the Earldom for your husband *and* yourself. Through your machinations, you hoped that Lord Blackmore would pass on the title to your husband, in the only way possible – by killing himself! For one cannot step aside from a title, once it has been assumed – it is held for life."

Lady Alderton only shrugged.

"And my name was chosen simply because you plucked me from the crowd and decided that I should be shamed alongside Lord Blackmore." Rachael shook her head. "How could you even think to do such a thing?"

"It was not meant to be personally injurious!" Lady Alderton cut the air with her hands. "I needed the name of a young lady, and yours was the first that I heard."

Silence followed this and Lady Alderton clapped her hands to her mouth, her eyes flaring wide as she realized, no doubt, what it was that she had said. Rachael offered her a small, sad smile, though her heart leaped wildly with relief.

"You have admitted it all, then," she said, as the crowd stared, as one, at Lady Alderton. "You are the one behind these rumors. You are the one who has sought to bring Lord Blackmore low, and you are the one who has offered the *ton* nothing but lies – both this Season and the last. Lord Blackmore holds no guilt, and no disgrace, bears no shame or question over his birth. Those lies came from your mouth, Lady Alderton, and they are revealed now, to us all."

CHAPTER FIFTEEN

"*Do* hurry."

Hugh rolled his eyes.

"I am not overly tardy. In case you have forgotten, I have been rather busy attempting to locate my brother."

Lord Elmsford shrugged.

"I am not unaware of that, though quite why that has made you take an age to prepare for the ball, I cannot know."

"Because I was finishing one or two letters," Hugh replied, a little sourly. "I have had two notes from two friends in Bath, both of whom said that they have seen no sign of my brother. I wrote to thank them and to beg them to inform me the very moment they see him, should they do so."

Lord Elmsford grinned.

"Come now, you know I am only jesting. I understand that these last few days have been very trying indeed, especially with the rumors continuing to fly around you."

Hugh grimaced at this and, giving himself one final glance in the mirror above the fireplace in the drawing room, nodded.

"I am prepared. Let us take our leave."

"Finally!" Lord Elmsford walked to the door, haste in his steps. "I am sure that Miss Simmons will be very glad to see you. I – oh."

Frowning, Hugh watched as Lord Elmsford stepped back, only for the butler to enter. He had been just about to knock as Lord Elmsford reached the door.

"Yes? What is it?"

"Your brother, my Lord."

Hugh's mouth fell open but, before he could even exclaim, the familiar face of his younger brother came into view, and to Hugh's even greater astonishment, he fell on Hugh's neck and hugged him tightly.

"Alderton," Hugh managed to say, looking at Lord Elmsford with wide eyes. "Goodness, this is a surprise. I thought I told you to stay in Bath?"

Lord Alderton stepped back, though he grasped Hugh's hands for a moment.

"It is good to see you, brother."

There was a throatiness to his voice, one which spoke of a deep upset and Hugh's heart turned over in his chest. What had happened for his brother to arrive so unexpectedly?

"It is good to see you also." Glancing at Lord Elmsford, he shrugged. "If you wish to go to the ball, then please do, Elmsford. I will remain here for a little longer."

With a smile, Lord Elmsford stepped away from the

door, rather than go through it, the ball now clearly forgotten.

"Can I pour you a brandy, Alderton?"

"Thank you, Lord Elmsford," came the reply, Alderton recalling Lord Elmsford. "It has been a difficult few weeks, and to be in your company again, Blackmore, brings me a little relief. I did not know what else to do!"

"I am sorry to hear it." Taking the glass from Lord Elmsford, Hugh kept his gaze fixed on his brother. "I have been looking for you, Alderton. I wrote letters to see if someone might be able to spy you in Bath, but I had no success. Where have you been?"

Lord Alderton sniffed, took a sip of his brandy, and then sighed so heavily that his shoulders rounded.

"I have been looking for my wife."

Hugh's heart jumped in his chest, and he threw a look to Lord Elmsford who only frowned.

"You seek Lady Alderton?"

"Yes." Lifting his glass to his lips, Lord Alderton took another sip and then looked back directly at Hugh. "I was foolish in my marriage. I married a lady I thought was the most wonderful creature in the world, only to then find her to be a shrew. She was always nipping at my heels, telling me that I had done wrong in this or that. She was never satisfied with what we had, or what I chose to do. I know you think me foolish in many of my choices, brother, and I will not say that you are wrong, but Elizabeth – that is, Lady Alderton – had laughed and teased me about my jovial and often selfish behavior, even before we were married. She knew the sort of gentleman I was but also trusted that I cared for her, which I believed I did. Once we were wed, however, I continued on the same path as regards how I live and act, but she altered significantly. She did not realize that I bore only a courtesy title. In short, I do not think that she would have married me, had she realized that my elder brother was an Earl. No doubt she would have pursued you instead, for that is the sort of fickle, selfish creature that she is... only I did not see it until after we married."

Hugh caught the look of regret pulling down every part of his brother's features and felt his own heart soften with sympathy. Yes, his brother was a fool, and certainly he ought not to have rushed into matrimony with such haste, but there was clear upset and hurt in his heart. It would not be wise or right for him to berate Alderton at this point.

"You think that she is in London, then," he said, slowly, wondering now whether his brother had ever been involved in Lady Alderton's schemes, and beginning to doubt whether such a thing could be.

"I do not know." Lord Alderton's voice cracked. "I have searched all through Bath, written to almost everyone I know, and she is still absent! In desperation, I came to London in the hope that you might help me, though I am fully aware that I ask a great deal in such a thing."

Hugh put a hand on his brother's shoulder and looked him straight in the eye.

"The truth is, Alderton, that I know your wife is present here in London. I have seen her, though I have not been introduced to her, so have not had a single conversation as yet. However, if your wife has fair hair and brown eyes, then I believe it is one and the same person that I have seen."

In that one moment, everything about his brother seemed to change. Lord Alderton's hair stood on end, his eyes rounded, his face paled and the hand which gripped his glass began to shake.

"I thought that you would be pleased to know that you have found her."

"But what... what is she doing here in London?" Lord Alderton asked, ignoring Hugh's remark entirely. "There must be a purpose, a *reason* behind it. She has been away from my side for a long period and, before that, complained incessantly about how much she wished she had been a Countess rather than a Viscountess."

All that Hugh had considered finally drew to one, clarifying conclusion and he nodded slowly, looking back at his brother.

"Might I ask if she was absent from you last Season also?"

Lord Alderton frowned.

"Yes, but she wished to go to London for a short while and, given how strained things had been during the first few weeks of our marriage, I saw no difficulty in permitting her to depart. She returned to the estate a short while thereafter, though the following months were very difficult indeed. I suggested that we take some time in Bath – though I also wanted to come to London so that she might meet you – and she was amenable to the idea. However, once we arrived, she promptly disappeared, and I have looked for her ever since!" Running one hand over his forehead, he let out a slow breath and closed his eyes. "She is conniving, Blackmore. Whatever she is doing here, it will be for a purpose. I do not doubt that."

Lord Elmsford cleared his throat, glancing at Hugh.

"And you do not know as to what that purpose might be?"

Hugh watched his brother carefully as, with a shrug, he flung out both hands, one either side and then let them fall, by way of answer to Lord Elmsford. He knew his brother well, and one thing Alderton could not do was lie. He was much too honest – brutally so – about everything, and did not hold the truth back from anyone. That was why their father had despaired of him, why Hugh had given up on giving a single iota of his time to wondering what his brother was doing. Lord Alderton had always been quite happy to inform him of what he was currently engaged in, no matter what it was, and looking at him now, Hugh was quite certain that his brother spoke honestly.

He had no knowledge of any of this.

"Sit down, Alderton." Waiting until his brother had taken his seat, Hugh took his now empty glass from him and went to refill it. "There is a reason that I was looking for you, a reason that is both grave and of the utmost concern." Turning back, he handed the glass to his brother but, rather than standing and talking down to him, chose to sit back down himself. Seeing Lord Alderton's eyes fixed on his, worry etched into the gentle lines on his face, Hugh closed his eyes and fought to find the right words. "Since I came to Town, there have been rumors sweeping through London about me. Someone attempted to push me into a situation with a rather tenacious widow, and thereafter, there came a rumor that I was insolvent and had a great deal of debt owed to a gambling den. I acted against this by throwing a lavish ball but still, the rumors came! They involved one Miss Simmons also, which was most unfortunate. I came to her defense, and we are now betrothed… though that is a story for another time." Seeing his brother's eyes widen all the more, Hugh let out a slightly rueful laugh. "The most recent rumor is one that I am battling at present. It states that I am not the legitimate heir, that I am, in fact, not the true son of our father."

"But that is quite dreadful!" Wide eyes stared back at Hugh as he nodded slowly. "Who would say such a thing, and what purpose would they have behind it?"

"The purpose, I cannot speak to," Hugh replied, choosing his words with great care and speaking slowly as he thought. "The person who has been spreading rumors, I believe, is none other than Lady Alderton, your wife."

He watched as understanding of this news spread across his brother's face, the shock only halted by the brandy that Lord Alderton threw down his throat.

"Where is she?" he asked, though Hugh merely shrugged. "I must find her. I know why she is doing this."

"Why?" Lord Elmsford rose to pour yet more brandy into Lord Alderton's glass. "What possible reason could she have for doing something like this to your brother?"

Lord Alderton closed his eyes and shuddered violently.

"Because she wants the title," he said, hoarsely. "If she can push you into a place of such desperation that you feel the only way to salvage the family name is to give up the title, to kill yourself, so that it passes to me, then that is what she will do. I do not doubt that she would have been eager to make her way to your estate and to comfort you, should her rumors have succeeded in their endeavors. That comfort would have come by way of whispers and dark encouragements, however. Encouragements to give up what is already rightfully yours, to give up your life. And she would, most likely, have encouraged you to do something rash, so that your death might seem an accident, thus preventing the scandal of a definite suicide." Sitting a little further forward in his chair, Alderton's eyes widened. "I did not ever want such a thing, Blackmore! I would never seek a way to steal from you, and I most certainly would not ever wish your death!"

"I will admit to, for a short while at least, wondering if this was your action - and for that I apologize. I should have trusted you," Hugh admitted, with a small smile. "The only question now is what it is that we are to do!"

Lord Elmsford got to his feet.

"We must find Lady Alderton." Making his way to the door, he stopped and gestured to it. "And we must hurry."

With a frown, Hugh rose also but did not hurry over to the door.

"Why?"

"Because she may say something more," Lord Elmsford replied, with a touch of impatience in his voice. "I fully expect her to be at the ball and, with Miss Simmons there also, it would be best for us to make our way there as quickly as we can."

Agreeing with this, and seeing the truth in Lord Elmsford's worry about what could occur, Hugh looked to his brother.

"Will you join us, Alderton? I am sure that my valet could provide you with something to wear. We are almost the same size, and it will not take long."

Lord Alderton rose to his feet, his expression now set in a mask of determination, his eyes lit with a fresh, strong light.

"I should like to come and find my wife, yes," he stated. "Thank you, Blackmore."

"Of course." Ringing the bell, Hugh felt the first flurry of nervousness begin to rush through him. "We *will* find her, Alderton. And let us hope that, in doing so, we put an end to all that has been said and done against me."

"It shall be," his brother promised, firmly. "I will make sure of it."

Hugh made his way into the ballroom, his eyes going from left to right as he sought out either Miss Simmons or Lady Alderton. Neither of them caught his attention and, with Lord Elmsford on one side and his brother on the other, they continued to their left, making their way slowly from one side of the room to the other.

"There." Lord Elmsford nudged him, lifting his chin in the direction of a gathered group to one side of the ballroom. "Look. Something is happening over there."

Hugh nodded and, with a glance at his brother, made his way in the direction of the slowly growing gathering of both gentlemen and ladies – and it was not long before he heard a familiar voice.

"Yes, I *am* wed to that fool, Viscount Alderton. But he has no ambition, no desire for anything. Can you imagine what such a life is like? To discover that your husband is a gentleman who cares for nothing other than himself and whatever it is that *he* desires? No, I have better ambitions than he."

Hugh looked at his brother and saw how he dropped his head, clearly mortified at hearing his wife's voice.

"And thus, unsatisfied with your lot, you chose to try to push Lord Blackmore out of society, to ruin his name so that you and your husband might try to then take his place in society. What were you hoping for? To drive him to be a man so disgraced, so low in spirit that he would be easily convinced to give up his title by killing himself? So that your husband would take it in his place??"

Hurrying forward, Hugh came to stand just behind a gentleman and a smaller lady, permitting him to look through the crowd to see none other than Miss Simmons standing opposite Lady Alderton, speaking with a firmness which had his admiration for her building furiously.

"And what if I *did*?" Lady Alderton stated, her tone harsh and eyes narrowed. "We married in haste and I did not realize at the time that my husband bore only a courtesy title while his elder brother held the title of Earl. You can imagine my disappointment, particularly when Lord Alderton appeared to behave just as any oaf might!"

Hugh closed his eyes briefly, struggling to listen to the harsh way Lady Alderton spoke, when his brother – her husband – was standing alongside him. He could not imagine the pain that his brother felt at this moment.

Miss Simmons' voice continued to ring out clearly, her determination growing all the more.

"And thus, you attempted to come up with a way to gain the Earldom for your husband *and* yourself. Through your machinations, you hoped that Lord Blackmore would pass on the title to your husband, in the only way possible – by killing himself! For one cannot step aside from a title, once it has been assumed – it is held for life."

Looking at Lady Alderton, wondering if she would admit to such a thing, Hugh's jaw worked as the lady only lifted her shoulders and let them fall. That was no confirmation.

"And my name was chosen simply because you plucked me from the crowd and decided that I should be shamed alongside Lord Blackmore. How could you even think to do such a thing?"

Miss Simmons moved a little closer, her continued strength forcing the truth from Lady Alderton's lips – and Hugh let out a long, slow breath of both relief and sadness.

"It was not meant to be personally injurious!" Lady Alderton gestured wildly to Miss Simmons, her eyes flaring wide. "I needed the name of a young lady and yours was the first I heard."

A murmur ran around the crowd but neither Lady Alderton nor Miss Simmons looked at anyone. Instead, Miss Simmons shook her head and took a step back.

"You have admitted it all, then. You *are* the one

behind these rumors. You are the one who has sought to bring Lord Blackmore to despair, and you are the one who has offered the *ton* nothing but lies – both this Season and the last. Lord Blackmore holds no guilt and no disgrace, bears no shame or question over his birth. Those lies came from your mouth, Lady Alderton, and they are revealed now, to us all."

Nothing was said for some moments. Lady Alderton opened her mouth and then closed it again, her eyes wide and a trembling running through her frame. With a glance at the crowd, she looked here and there, only for her eyes to snag on none other than her husband.

"I have been looking for you for a long time, Elizabeth." The crowd parted, the group separating as Lord Alderton stepped forward, walking through them towards his wife. "It seems that you have been pursuing your own dark ends while I have remained oblivious to it all."

"My brother had no part to play in any of this." Seeing now that the crowd might turn on Alderton should he not say anything, Hugh made his way forward also, catching the attention of the *ton*. Miss Simmons too turned to him and, with a brief smile, he offered her his arm. Without a word, she took it at once, standing as close to him as she could. "My brother appeared this very evening at my house, having spent weeks searching for his wife. Exhausted, broken-hearted, and sorrowful, he and I have come to the same conclusion as Miss Simmons. It is only by Miss Simmons' strength, determination, and wisdom, however, that we have heard the truth from your lips, Lady Alderton."

Lady Alderton was shaking visibly by this point, looking from her husband to Hugh and then back again. She could say nothing, her eyes flaring wide, one hand going to her mouth as everything she had built, everything she had hoped would occur, came tumbling down around her.

"You and I have never been acquainted," Hugh continued, speaking now more for the benefit of the group around them who would, no doubt, go and speak to everyone they knew about what they had witnessed, once it had all come to an end. "I did not know your face, and I had never heard your title given to me. You were able, then, to move about London society as a stranger to me. The darkness of your intentions, the selfishness of your actions, and your wickedness is more than I can even comprehend and, at this juncture, I must also say how sorry I am for my brother, than he ever thought you would make him a suitable bride. I can see the pain and the suffering you have caused him, and that is sorrowful to me indeed."

"There is always divorce," Lord Alderton muttered, and while that brought many a gasp of both shock and astonishment, Hugh could understand his brother's desire for such a thing, regardless of the scandal it might cause. "For the moment, brother, let me take my wife from this place and remove her from your presence at once. You have endured enough, and I am only sorry for my part in it."

Hugh put his hand to his brother's shoulder.

"You had no part in it."

Lord Alderton looked up miserably.

"I did not marry well. I was much too hasty, and it was foolishness which led me to that. Forgive me, brother."

"There is nothing to forgive," Hugh promised, not once looking at Lady Alderton. "Come and speak with me tomorrow."

Having received his brother's promise that he would do so, Hugh turned again to Miss Simmons, noting that the crowd was finally beginning to disperse.

"My wonderful Rachael," he murmured, seeing her eyes glistening with tears. "How strong you were. Your determination and your wisdom, as I have said, is what has brought this all to an end. I do not think that I am worthy of you!"

Miss Simmons leaned into him and, caring little for those who remained, buried her face into his chest. Hugh wrapped his arms around her and held her close, feeling the shuddering breath that escaped from her as the tension and strain began to fade away.

"It is over," he promised as she looked up at him again, wishing desperately that he might press a kiss to her lips. "It is at an end. Your reputation *and* my own are restored and all that waits for us now is happiness."

EPILOGUE

Rachael pulled herself away from the window and hurried back to her chair. She stood in front of it as though she had only just risen from her seat, rather than come back from hovering by the window, waiting for the arrival of Lord Blackmore.

After last evening – and with the relief of knowing that Rachael's reputation was now fully restored – her mother had promised her a few minutes alone with her betrothed, and Rachael had been nothing but impatient in waiting for his arrival. Last evening had been an incredibly difficult night, but Rachael had felt nothing but utter relief at its conclusion. There had been much she wished to share with Lord Blackmore, and she had wanted nothing more than to rest in his embrace, but there had been no opportunity for that. Instead, she had walked arm in arm with her betrothed, but had been stopped often to accept murmurs of apology from various members of the *ton*. It had been a strange relief to hear such things said to her and the more they had gone on, the more her heart had filled with happiness.

"Lord Blackmore, my Lady."

The butler had not even left the room before Rachael had hurried across to Lord Blackmore and, as his arms opened, stepped into his embrace and held him tightly. They said nothing for some moments, the sweet relief of simply being in each other's company again all that they needed. Rachael closed her eyes and set one hand to his chest, just above his heart, while the other went around his neck, pulling her as close to him as she could manage.

"I am so very glad to see you again, my love."

Lifting her head, Rachael looked straight up into his eyes, smiling at him.

"My heart has been yearning for your arrival," she told him, honestly. "I have been able to think of nothing else."

"Nor I."

Bending his head, he kissed her lightly, and Rachael lost herself in his embrace, the sweetness of it overwhelming her. The gentle kiss gained a little more strength as she swept both arms around his neck, feeling his hands tighten around her waist.

Lord Blackmore broke the kiss with a quiet groan of evident frustration, and Rachael blushed, burying her face in his neck for a moment.

"I dare not continue for fear that your mother or father will come in, and think me quite the scoundrel!"

Rachael laughed, the sound a little muffled before, finally, stepping back out of his arms.

"My mother was glad to give us a few minutes alone. How do you fare after yesterday evening?"

Lord Blackmore still held her hand in his as, together, they walked to sit down on the couch. His eyes searched hers for a few moments before he answered, beginning with a long, heavy breath.

"It was all rather astonishing," he said, eventually. "My brother's sudden appearance, the truth about his wife... it was almost too incredible to hear. But thereafter, to see my brother's pain and to understand the cause behind it was very difficult to take in. The look on his face as he heard his wife speaking of him in such an unkind manner is not something I shall ever be able to forget."

Rachael's heart squeezed painfully.

"I am sorry for that," she answered, as Lord Blackmore held her gaze. "I cannot imagine the suffering he is enduring at present."

"He came to the house last evening, very late indeed." Lord Blackmore shook his head and sighed, passing one hand over his eyes. "He had nowhere to stay and begged to reside with me until he could understand what he will do. His wife would not let him stay at her lodgings, and neither would she admit to any fault. Apparently, she was doing all she could to justify her actions, and my brother could not tolerate anything further."

Rachael's eyes flared.

"What will happen now?"

"I do not know." As he looked away, Lord Blackmore's jaw worked. "Lady Alderton has caused my brother more suffering than he can endure. My brother has always been less than wise, I will admit, but this situation has forced him to consider a great many things. I do not know what he will do next, but I have assured him that, whatever it is he should choose, I will be with him, and support him in whatever decision he reaches."

"You are a gentleman with excellent character," Rachael murmured, squeezing his hand gently. "I do hope that your brother will recover from this."

"He will. In time." Lord Blackmore's smile began to grow. "And we must also consider ourselves and our good fortune. After all, we have not only recovered our reputations but there is also the promise of a joyous future for us as husband and wife! Finally, I can set this matter to the side and look instead to what is to come next – a life with you."

Rachael smiled at him, her own heart beginning to quicken as she thought of what was to come.

"My mother has already finished preparing my trousseau. The banns will be called very soon, I think."

"Within a fortnight," he told her, making her heart leap with excitement. "And then, after three Sundays have passed, we shall stand up together to become husband and wife. What think you of that?"

Laughing softly, Rachael shifted a little in her seat, moving closer to him.

"I think it the most wonderful thing in all the world," she answered, softly, seeing his eyes gentle with tenderness. "You know how much I have come to care for you, do you not?"

"Mayhap I do, mayhap I have forgotten." His lips

quirked as she flushed, his fingers threading through hers. "Why do you not remind me, however? That way, I shall be certain to remember."

The heat in her face did not leave but, all the same, she looked up into his eyes and pressed her hand against his cheek.

"When we were first acquainted, I did not think, for even a single moment, that it would ever come to this." Her lips pulled into a light smile. "Or that we would go through so much difficulty!"

"Nor I."

"But though I would not say that I am grateful for what we have been forced to endure, I *am* thankful that the circumstances have brought us together, to a place where we now look to our future with happiness and love in our hearts." Taking a deep breath, she set her hand on his shoulder and looked into his eyes. "I do love you, Blackmore."

Lord Blackmore searched her eyes, his smile beginning to creep up slowly as if he were only just beginning to understand what it was that she had said. Rachael's heart began to pound all the more quickly, but Lord Blackmore lifted his hand, took hers as it sat on his shoulder, and bringing it to his lips, kissed the back of her hand gently.

"I adore you." Lifting his eyes to hers again, he squeezed her fingers gently. "When I told the *ton* we were betrothed, I spoke without thinking – but I am glad now that I spoke as I did. It has brought me to you, and you to me, and I promise you, from this day forward, I shall love you with my whole heart, Rachael. You have become so precious to me that I wish to spend every day, every *moment* with you. Our wedding day seems much too far away!"

She laughed softly at this, understanding precisely what he meant.

"Just a little longer, my love, and we shall be husband and wife."

"And what a happy, joyous day that will be," he told her, smiling. "The day I take my love into my arms and promise never to let her go."

Rachael and Lord Blackmore found each other! Let's wish them happy!

Check out my next Wallflower book now on preorder!

The Wallflower's Secret

Did you miss the first book in the Waltzing with Wallflowers series? The Wallflower's Unseen Charm Read ahead for a sneak peek of the story of a wallflower who can't keep quiet!

MY DEAR READER

Thank you for reading and supporting my books! I hope this story brought you some escape from the real world into the always captivating Regency world. A good story, especially one with a happy ending, just brightens your day and makes you feel good! If you enjoyed the book, would you leave a review on Amazon? Reviews are always appreciated.

Below is a complete list of all my books! Why not click and see if one of them can keep you entertained for a few hours?

The Duke's Daughters Series
The Duke's Daughters: A Sweet Regency Romance Boxset
A Rogue for a Lady
My Restless Earl
Rescued by an Earl
In the Arms of an Earl
The Reluctant Marquess (Prequel)

A Smithfield Market Regency Romance
The Smithfield Market Romances: A Sweet Regency Romance Boxset
The Rogue's Flower

Saved by the Scoundrel
Mending the Duke
The Baron's Malady

The Returned Lords of Grosvenor Square
The Returned Lords of Grosvenor Square: A Regency Romance Boxset
The Waiting Bride
The Long Return
The Duke's Saving Grace
A New Home for the Duke

The Spinsters Guild
The Spinsters Guild: A Sweet Regency Romance Boxset
A New Beginning
The Disgraced Bride
A Gentleman's Revenge
A Foolish Wager
A Lord Undone

Convenient Arrangements
Convenient Arrangements: A Regency Romance Collection
A Broken Betrothal
In Search of Love
Wed in Disgrace
Betrayal and Lies
A Past to Forget
Engaged to a Friend

Landon House

Landon House: A Regency Romance Boxset
Mistaken for a Rake
A Selfish Heart
A Love Unbroken
A Christmas Match
A Most Suitable Bride
An Expectation of Love

Second Chance Regency Romance
Second Chance Regency Romance Boxset
Loving the Scarred Soldier
Second Chance for Love
A Family of her Own
A Spinster No More

Soldiers and Sweethearts
Soldiers and Sweethearts Boxset
To Trust a Viscount
Whispers of the Heart
Dare to Love a Marquess
Healing the Earl
A Lady's Brave Heart

Ladies on their Own: Governesses and Companions
Ladies on their Own Boxset
More Than a Companion
The Hidden Governess
The Companion and the Earl
More than a Governess
Protected by the Companion

Lost Fortunes, Found Love
Lost Fortunes, Found Love Boxset
A Viscount's Stolen Fortune
For Richer, For Poorer
Her Heart's Choice
A Dreadful Secret
Their Forgotten Love
His Convenient Match

Only for Love
The Heart of a Gentleman
A Lord or a Liar
The Earl's Unspoken Love
The Viscount's Unlikely Ally
The Highwayman's Hidden Heart
Miss Millington's Unexpected Suitor

Waltzing with Wallflowers
The Wallflower's Unseen Charm
The Wallflower's Midnight Waltz
Wallflower Whispers

Christmas Stories
The Uncatchable Earl
Love and Christmas Wishes: Three Regency Romance Novellas
A Family for Christmas
Mistletoe Magic: A Regency Romance
Heart, Homes & Holidays: A Sweet Romance Anthology

Christmas Kisses Series

Christmas Kisses Box Set
The Lady's Christmas Kiss
The Viscount's Christmas Queen
Her Christmas Duke

Happy Reading!
    All my love,
      Rose

A SNEAK PEEK OF THE WALLFLOWER'S UNSEEN CHARM

PROLOGUE

"You must promise me that you will *try*."

Miss Joy Bosworth rolled her eyes at her mother.

"Try to be more like my elder sisters, yes? That *is* what you mean, is it not?"

"And what is wrong with being like them?" Lady Halifax's stern tone told Joy in no uncertain terms that to criticize Bettina, Sarah, and Mary – all three of whom had married within the last few years – was a very poor decision indeed. Wincing, Joy fell silent and dropped her gaze to her lap as her beleaguered lady's maid continued to fix her hair. This was the third time that her lady's maid had set her hair, for the first two attempts had been deemed entirely unsuitable by Joy's mother – though quite what was wrong with it, Joy had been completely unable to see.

"You are much too forward, too quick to give your opinion," her mother continued, gazing at Joy's reflection in the looking glass, her eyes narrowing a little. "All of your elder sisters are quiet, though Bettina perhaps a little too much so, but their husbands greatly appreciate that about them! They speak when they are asked to speak, give their opinion when it is desired and otherwise say very little when it comes to matters which do not concern them. *You,* on the other hand, speak when you are *not* asked to do so, give your opinion most readily, and say a great deal on *any* subject even when it does not concern you!"

Hearing the strong emphasis, Joy chose not to drop her head further, as her mother might have expected, but instead to lift her chin and look back steadily. She was not about to be cowed when it came to such a trait. In some ways, she was rather proud of her determination to speak as she thought, for she was the only one of her sisters who did so. Mayhap it was simply because she was the youngest, but Joy did not truly know why - she had always been determined to speak up for herself and, simply because she was in London, was not, she thought, cause to alter herself now!

"You must find a suitable husband!" Exclaiming aloud, Lady Halifax threw up her hands, perhaps seeing the glint of steel in Joy's eyes. "Continuing to behave as you are will not attract anyone to you, I can assure you of that!"

"The *right* gentleman would still be attracted," Joy shot back, adding her own emphasis. "There must be some amongst society who do not feel the same way as you, Mother. I do not seek to disagree with you, only to suggest that there might be a little more consideration in some, or even a different viewpoint altogether!"

"I know what I am talking about!" Lady Halifax smote Joy gently on the shoulder though her expression was one of frustration. "I have already had three daughters wed and it would do you well to listen to me and my advice."

Joy did not know what to say. Yes, she had listened to her mother on many an occasion, but that did not mean that she had to take everything her mother said to heart... and on this occasion, she was certain that Lady Halifax was quite wrong.

"If I am not true to who I am, Mama, then will that not make for a very difficult marriage?"

"A difficult marriage?" This was said with such a degree of astonishment that Joy could not help but smile. "There is no such thing as a difficult marriage, not unless one of the two parties *within* the marriage itself attempts to make it so. Do you not understand, Joy? I am telling you to alter yourself so that you do *not* cause any difficulties, both for yourself now, and for your husband in the future."

The smile on Joy's face slipped and then blew away, her forehead furrowing as she looked at her mother again. Lady Halifax was everything a lady of quality ought to be, and she had trained each of her daughters to be as she was... except that Joy had never been the success her other daughters had been. Even now, the thought of stepping into marriage with a gentleman she barely knew, simply because he was deemed suitable, was rather horrifying to Joy, and was made all the worse by the idea that she would somehow have to pretend to be someone she was not!

"As I have said, Joy, you will try."

This time, Joy realized, it was not a question her mother had been asking her but a statement. A statement which said that she was expected to do nothing other than what her mother said – and to do so without question also.

I shall not lie.

"I think my hair is quite presentable now, Mama." Steadfastly refusing to either agree with or refuse what her mother had said, Joy sat up straight in her chair, her head lifting, her shoulders dropping low as she turned her head from side to side. "Very elegant, I must say."

"The ribbon is not the right color."

Joy resisted the urge to roll her eyes for what would be the second time.

"Mama, it is a light shade of green and it is threaded through the many braids Clara has tied my hair into. It is quite perfect and cannot be faulted. Besides, it does match the gown perfectly. You made certain of that yourself."

So saying, she threw a quick smile to her lady's maid and saw a twitch of Clara's lips before the maid bowed her head, stepping back so that Lady Halifax would not see the smile on her face.

"It is not quite as I would want it, but it will have to do." Lady Halifax sniffed and waved one hand in Clara's direction. "My daughter requires her gown now. And be quick about it, we are a little short on time."

"If you had not insisted that Clara do my hair on two further occasions, then we would not be in danger of being tardy," Joy remarked, rising from her chair, and walking across the room, quite missing the flash in her mother's eyes. "It was quite suitable the first time."

"*I* shall be the judge of that," came the sharp retort, as Lady Halifax stalked to the door. "Now do hurry up. The carriage is waiting, and I do not want us to bring the attention of the entire *ton* down upon us by walking in much later than any other!"

Joy sighed and nodded, turning back to where Clara was ready with her gown. Coming to London and seeking out a suitable match was not something she could get the least bit excited about, and this ball, rather than being a momentous one, filled with hope and expectation, felt like a heaviness on her shoulders. The sooner it was over, Joy considered, the happier she would be.

CHAPTER ONE

"And Lord Granger is seated there."
"Mm-hm."
Nudging Joy lightly, her mother scowled.
"You are not paying the least bit of attention! Instead, you are much too inclined towards staring! Though quite what you are staring at, I cannot imagine!"

Joy tilted her head but did not take her eyes away from what she had been looking at.

"I was wondering whether that lady there – the one with the rather ornate hairstyle – found it difficult to wear such a thing without difficulty or pain." The lady in question had what appeared to be a bird's nest of some description, adorned with feathers and lace, planted on one side of her head, with her hair going through it as though it were a part of the creation. There was also a bird sitting on the edge of the nest, though to Joy's eyes, it looked rather monstrous and not at all as it ought. "Surely it must be stuck to her head in some way." She could not keep a giggle back when the lady curtsied and then rose, only for her magnificent headpiece to wobble terribly. "Oh dear, perhaps it is not as well secured as it ought to be!"

"Will you stop speaking so loudly?"

The hiss from Lady Halifax had Joy's attention snapping back to her mother, a slight flush touching the edge of her cheeks as she realized that one or two of the other ladies near them were glancing in her direction. She had spoken a little too loudly for both her own good and her mother's liking.

"My apologies, Mama."

"I should think so!" Lady Halifax grabbed Joy's arm in a somewhat tight grip and then began to walk in the opposite direction of that taken by the lady with the magnificent hair. "Pray do not embarrass both me and yourself, with your hasty tongue!"

"I do not mean to," Joy muttered, allowing her mother to take her in whatever direction she wished. "I simply speak as I think."

"A trait I ought to have worked out of you by now, but instead, it seems determined to cling to you!" With a sigh, Lady Halifax shook her head. "Now look, do you see there?"

Coming to a hasty stop, Joy looked across the room, following the direction of her mother's gaze. "What is it that you wish me to look at, Mama?"

"Those young ladies there," came the reply. "Do you see them? They stand clustered together, hidden in the shadows of the ballroom. Even their own mothers or sponsors have given up on them!"

A frown tugged at Joy's forehead.

"I do not know what you are speaking of Mama."

"The wallflowers!" Lady Halifax turned sharply to Joy, her eyes flashing. "Do you not see them? They stand there, doing nothing other than adorning the wall. They are passed over constantly, ignored by the gentlemen of the *ton,* who care very little for their company."

"Then that is the fault of the gentlemen of the *ton,*" Joy answered, a little upset by her mother's remarks. "I do not think it is right to blame the young ladies for such a thing."

Lady Halifax groaned aloud, closing her eyes.

"Why do you willfully misunderstand? They are not wallflowers by choice, but because they are deemed as unsuitable for marriage, for one reason or another."

"Which, again, might not be their own doing."

"Perhaps, but all the same," Lady Halifax continued, sounding more exasperated than ever, "I have shown you these young ladies as a warning."

Joy's eyebrows shot towards her hairline.

"A warning?"

"Yes, that you will yourself become one such young lady if you do not begin to behave yourself and act as you ought." Moving so that she faced Joy directly, Lady Halifax narrowed her eyes a little. "You will find yourself standing there with them, doing nothing other than watching the gentlemen of London take various *other* young ladies out to dance, rather than showing any genuine interest in you. Would that not be painful? Would that not trouble you?"

The answer her mother wished her to give was evident to Joy, but she could not bring herself to say it. It was not that she wanted to cause her mother any pain, but that she could not permit herself to be false, not even if it would bring her a little comfort.

"It might," she admitted, eventually, as Lady Halifax let out another stifled groan, clearly exasperated. "But as I have said before, Mama, I do not wish to be courted by a gentleman who is unaware of my true nature. I do not see why I should hide myself away, simply so that I can please a suitor. If such a thing were to happen, if I were to be willing to act in that way, it would not make for a happy arrangement. Sooner or later, my real self would return to the fore, and then what would my husband do? It is not as though he could step back from our marriage. Therefore, I would be condemning both him and myself, to a life of misery. I do not think that would be at all agreeable."

"That is where you are wrong." Lady Halifax lifted her chin, though she looked straight ahead. "To be wed is the most satisfactory situation one can find oneself in, regardless of the circumstances. It is not as though you will spend a great deal of time with your husband so, therefore, you will never need to reveal your 'true nature', as you put it."

The more her mother talked, the more Joy found herself growing almost despondent, such was the picture Lady Halifax was painting of what would be waiting for her. She understood that yes, she was here to find a suitable match, but to then remove to her husband's estate, where she would spend most of her days alone and only be in her husband's company whenever he desired it, did not seem to Joy to be a very pleasant circumstance. That would be very dull indeed, would it not? Her existence would become small, insignificant, and utterly banal, and that was certainly *not* the future Joy wanted for herself.

"Now, do lift your head up, stand tall, and smile," came the command. "We must go and speak to Lord Falconer and Lord Dartford at once."

Joy hid her sigh by lowering her head, her eyes squeezing closed for a few moments. There was no time to protest, however, no time to explain to her mother that what had just been discussed had settled Joy's mind against such things as this, for Lady Halifax once more marched Joy across the room and, before she knew it, introduced Joy to the two gentlemen whom she had pointed out, as well as to one Lady Dartford, who was Lord Dartford's mother.

"Good evening." Joy rose from her curtsey and tried to smile, though her smile was a little lackluster. "How very glad I am to make your acquaintance."

"Said quite perfectly." Lord Dartford chuckled, his dark eyes sweeping across her features, then dropping down to her frame as Joy blushed furiously. "So, you are next in line to try your hand at the marriage mart?"

"Next in line?"

"Yes." Lord Dartford waved a hand as though to dismiss her words and her irritation, which Joy had attempted to make more than evident by the sweep of her eyebrow. "You have three elder sisters do you not?"

"Yes, I do." Joy kept her eyebrows lifted. "All of whom are all now wed and settled."

"And now you must do the same." Lord Dartford chuckled, but Joy did not smile. The sound was not a pleasant one. "Unfortunately, none of your sisters were able to catch my eye and, alas, I do not think that you will be able to do so either."

"Dartford!"

His mother's gasp of horror was clear, but Joy merely smiled, her stomach twisting at the sheer arrogance which the gentleman had displayed.

"That is a little forward of you, Lord Dartford," she remarked, speaking quite clearly, and ignoring the way that her mother set one hand to the small of her back in clear warning. "What is to say that I would have any interest in *your* company?"

This response wiped the smile from Lord Dartford's face. His dark eyes narrowed, and his jaw set but, much to Joy's delight, his friend began to guffaw, slapping Lord Dartford on the shoulder.

"You have certainly been set in your place!" Lord Falconer laughed as Joy looked back into Lord Dartford's angry expression without flinching. "And the lady is quite right, that was one of the most superior things I have heard you say this evening!"

"Only this evening?" Enjoying herself far too much, Joy tilted her head and let a smile dance across her features. "Again, Lord Dartford, I ask you what difference it would make to me to have a gentleman such as yourself interested in furthering their acquaintance with me? It is not as though I must simply accept every gentleman who comes to seek me out, is it? And I can assure you, I certainly would not accept you!"

Lord Falconer laughed again but Lord Dartford's

eyes narrowed all the more, his jaw tight and his frame stiff with clear anger and frustration.

"I do not think a young lady such as yourself should display such audacity, Miss Bosworth."

"And if I want your opinion, Lord Dartford, then I will ask you for it," Joy shot back, just as quickly. "Thus far, I do not recall doing so."

"We must excuse ourselves."

The hand that had been on Joy's back now turned into a pressing force that propelled her away from Lord Dartford, Lord Falconer, and Lady Dartford – the latter of whom was standing, staring at Joy with wide eyes, her face a little pale.

"Do excuse us."

Lady Halifax inclined her head and then took Joy's hand, grasping it tightly rather than with any gentleness whatsoever, dragging her away from the gentlemen she had only just introduced Joy to.

"Mama, you are hurting me!" Pulling her hand away, Joy scowled when her mother rounded on her. "Please, you must stop–"

"Do you know what you have done?"

The hissed words from her mother had Joy stopping short, a little surprised at her mother's vehemence.

"I have done nothing other than speak my mind and set Lord Dartford – someone who purports to be a gentleman – back into his place. I do not know what makes him think that I would have *any* interest in–"

"News of this will spread through London!" Lady Halifax blinked furiously, and it was only then that Joy saw the tears in her mother's eyes. "This is your very first ball on the eve of your come out, and you decide to speak with such force and impudence to the Earl of Dartford?"

A writhing began to roll itself around Joy's stomach.

"I do not know what you mean. I did nothing wrong."

"It is not about wrong or right," came the reply, as Lady Halifax whispered with force towards Joy. "It is about wisdom. You did not speak with any wisdom this evening, and now news of what you did will spread throughout society. Lady Dartford will see to that."

Joy lifted her shoulders and then let them fall.

"I could not permit Lord Dartford to speak to me in such a way. I am worthy of respect, am I not?"

"You could have ignored him!" Lady Halifax threw up her hands, no longer managing to maintain her composure, garnering the attention of one or two others nearby. "You did not have to say a single thing! A simple look – or a slight curl of the lip – would have sufficed. Instead, you did precisely what I told you not to do and now news of your audacity will spread through London. Lady Dartford is one of the most prolific gossips in all of London and given that you insulted her son, I fear for what she will say."

Joy kept her chin lifted.

"Mama, Lady Dartford was shocked at her own son's remarks to me."

"But that does not mean that she will speak of *him* in the same way that she will speak of you," Lady Halifax told her, a single tear falling as red spots appeared on her cheeks. "Do you not understand, Joy?"

"Lord Falconer laughed at what I said."

Lady Halifax closed her eyes.

"That means nothing, other than the fact that he found your remarks and your behavior to be mirthful. It will not save your reputation."

"I did nothing to ruin my reputation."

"Oh, but you did." A flash came into her mother's eyes. "You may not see it as yet, but I can assure you, you have done yourself a great deal of damage. I warned you, I *asked* you to be cautious and instead, you did the opposite. Now, within the first ball of the Season, your sharp tongue and your determination to speak as you please has brought you into greater difficulty than you can imagine." Her eyes closed, a heavy sigh breaking from her. "Mayhap you will become a wallflower after all."

Hmm, my mother always said my mouth would get me into trouble…and now Miss Bosworth could be in trouble! Check out the rest of the story on the Kindle store The Wallflower's Unseen Charm

JOIN MY MAILING LIST

Sign up for my newsletter to stay up to date on new releases, contests, giveaways, freebies, and deals!

Free book with signup!

Monthly Facebook Giveaways! Books and Amazon gift cards!
Join me on Facebook: https://www.facebook.com/rosepearsonauthor

Website: www.RosePearsonAuthor.com

Follow me on Goodreads: Author Page

You can also follow me on Bookbub!
Click on the picture below – see the Follow button?

228 | JOIN MY MAILING LIST

Printed by Amazon Italia Logistica S.r.l.
Torrazza Piemonte (TO), Italy